ONE NIGHT IN COPÁN

CHRONICLES OF MADNESS FORETOLD

TALES OF MYSTERY, FANTASY AND HORROR

W. E. GUTMAN

CCB Publishing
British Columbia, Canada

One Night in Copán:
Chronicles of Madness Foretold, Tales of Mystery, Fantasy and Horror

Copyright ©2012 by W. E. Gutman
ISBN-13 978-1-77143-016-6
First Edition

Library and Archives Canada Cataloguing in Publication
Gutman, W. E., 1937-
One night in Copán : chronicles of madness foretold, tales of mystery, fantasy and
horror / written by W. E. Gutman – 1st ed.
ISBN 978-1-77143-016-6
Also available in electronic format.
Additional cataloguing data available from Library and Archives Canada

Photo and cover design by the author.

This book is printed on acid-free paper.

This is largely a work of fiction. Allusions to real persons, living or dead, and the
dramatization of actual events are meant to lend the narrative epic realism. All other
characters and events are fictitious or fictionalized.

Publisher: CCB Publishing
             British Columbia, Canada
             www.ccbpublishing.com

FOR LINDA

Also by W. E. GUTMAN

JOURNEY TO XIBALBA -- The Subversion of Human Rights in Central America © 2000. Reporter's Notebook (out of print).

NOCTURNES -- Tales from the Dreamtime
© 2006. Surrealistic fiction.

FLIGHT FROM EIN SOF
© 2009. Satire.

THE INVENTOR
© 2009. Historical fiction.

A PALER SHADE OF RED: Memoirs of a Radical.
© 2012. Autobiography.

ONE LAST DREAM. Screenplay (English-language version). Registered 2010 with the American Writers' Guild. © 2012.

UN DERNIER RÊVE. Screenplay (French-language version; translated by the author). © 2012.

CONTENTS

Evil has a wandering, fluid quality;
It drifts like thought.
Lance Morrow

PROLOGUE

I can calculate the motion of heavenly bodies,
but not the madness of people.
Isaac Newton

There exist ill-defined forms of mental illness, so subtle, so skillfully concealed and so utterly undetectable that they elude even those trained to recognize the myriad faces behind which they hide. Is he demented who pretends to be sane? Is he who fakes madness -- mad? Is conformist behavior proof of sanity? Is a clown "crazy?" Would his buffoonery be sanctioned outside the circus tent? He's only play-acting, you say? What about motorists who willfully exceed the speed limit: are they clear-headed? Are citizens who, time after time rush to the polls and vote into office inept or corrupt politicians under the ludicrous pretext that they're taking part in the "democratic process" -- in full possession of their faculties? Or are they imbeciles who deserve the scoundrels they helped elect?

Is the soldier who fires at an enemy he can't see behaving rationally or, to dilute the horror (or ease his conscience), is he pretending to be shooting blanks every time he squeezes the trigger? If not, if he finds moral justification in sanctioned murder -- or derives some secret thrill from it -- is he demented, evil or just a hopeless moron?

Are boxers who bash each-others' brains out -- for money -- out of their minds? Would their fights-to-the-finish seem less brutish if they didn't appear to enjoy themselves so much? Aren't the fans who salivate at the prospect of blood, of a bone-crushing knockout, equally deranged?

Are the uninvited evangelists who compel "primitive" peoples to cover their breasts and genitals "for the love of God," who force-feed guileless children alien concepts and rob cultures of their identity, sane or dangerous psychopaths further unhinged by religious zeal?

Listen to the maniacal soul-robbers who harangue their congregations. Look at the transfixed masses of 'born-again' who sway and swing and rock, their arms outstretched toward heaven as they pray for the cleansing firestorms of apocalypse. Are they out of their minds or the unwitting victims of mass-hysteria?

What about the "prophets"? Were they merely confused talking heads or cunning terrorists; clueless prognosticators or schemers blinded by their own fury; soothsayers and mystic diviners who spoke in riddles and esoteric babble or crafty politicians bent on sowing fear in the hearts of the masses? Were their intentions noble or did they suffer from acute megalomania, monomania, egomania and thanatomania -- a consuming preoccupation with death? Wouldn't they all have been diagnosed as certifiably insane -- or called charlatans -- had modern psychiatry not spinelessly declined to see them as superstitious crackpots pickled in gooey mysticism and predisposed to treat all inexplicable natural phenomena as the manifestation of some unknowable, invisible spirit?

Aren't the dream merchants, the demagogue-pedagogues and the healers, the petty bureaucrats, the would-be public servants and the corporate kingpins who deconstruct reality and peddle cheap imitations of Utopia -- insufferable psychopaths?

If men were put away for their natural tendencies (or for the habits and fixations they pick up along the way) prisons and mental hospitals would be bursting at the seams. Madness is somehow less reprehensible when it festers in high places; when ruthless entrepreneurs are eulogized for their "initiative" and their cunning; when my-country-right-or-wrong "patriots" brush aside lies, rationalize injustice, defend sleaze and political chicanery; when fanatical evangelism is hyped as "God's work;" when fraudulent and unwinnable wars that only enrich bankers and cannon merchants are waged far from home in the name of "national security;" and when freedom of thought is condemned as heresy and all moral codes are rescinded to protect the interests of the moneyed elite.

Pray tell, who are the mad, and who are the meek who inherit the wind? A slight detour to the brink might help tell them apart. There's more to madness than meets the eye. Let me count the ways.

PART ONE
THE TALES

IN DRANOMOS

A desert is a place without expectations.
Nadine Gordimer

It began with the birds. Dead birds. Dead grackle chicks. Had they tumbled out of their nest? Were they ousted by greedy siblings, dislodged by marauding ravens and beaked to death? Was it Shadow, the itinerant tomcat, the elusive feral feline that kept tongues wagging well after backyard gossip had turned to very small talk? The grackles' eye sockets had been picked clean, their belly feathers plucked as if in haste, their slender legs broken at the knees. They lay there on the concrete patio, four of them, disfigured, stilled, frozen in time.

Then there was the dead lizard at the bottom of the pool, a ten-inch striped little beauty with long, willowy digits and an endearing expression. I'd used a fine-mesh net at the end of a long pole to bring it to the surface, and I'd examined it for signs of life. There were none. The graceful reptile's eyes were shut. Saddened, I'd cupped it in my hand for a while. Sadness turned to unease. I buried it in the shade of a honeysuckle bush.

No, it wasn't superstition, legend or a penchant for mysticism that triggered the disquiet, the premonitions. Many years earlier I'd come upon a dying seagull, a stately old bird that flapped its wings listlessly, its lifeless eyes turned skyward as it gasped for one last breath of sea air. The sight of the expiring ace flier had filled me with sorrow; it also produced a numbing fear I'd never known. I remember getting chills, feeling the hair on the back of my neck bristle as if caressed by a sudden, icy gust.

Six months later, my mother died of pancreatic cancer. It'd taken months of pain -- constant, searching, tenacious. She'd turned yellow, gone bald, shed half her weight and slowly lost her mind. I'd witnessed this irreversible transformation with disbelief, helplessness, anger. Our evasions and lies had kept her hoping, fighting at first. Then she'd given up. One day, when the others left the room to stretch their legs after an all-night vigil, I'd touched her face and called her name.

"Mama, mama, don't go."

She'd winced and her eyelids had parted ever so briefly, revealing cloudy, swollen, lifeless orbs, like those of the moribund seagull. I knew she'd seen me, felt my presence, heard the words I'd whispered. She expired that evening. June was young and the air was filled with spring's heady bouquet. A seagull flew by. Every vestige of childhood in me died with my mother that day. Only the dreams she'd dreamed for me survived, some as yet unfulfilled, others beyond reach except in the limitless regions of a mother's love.

I'd cursed her. No one understood the rage that surged within me. I felt betrayed, lost, abandoned. Taken for granted, often unnoticed in life, longed for in death, my mother would have been the first to grasp this paradox. No one else did, not even my father who, familiar with the contradictions of the human soul, had failed to recognize in his son's calumnies the brittle fragments of a broken heart. Heeding her last wishes, we'd buried her ashes in a family plot where grandma Henrietta and Uncle Johnny would later be laid to rest. It'd rained that day; it would rain every time I came to the cemetery. And I'd grumbled because my shoes had gotten wet and caked with mud. It's the nature of coincidence to deliver a hint of irony.

All during my mother's ordeal, and after her death I'd harked back to that fateful winter morning stroll on the beach when the majestic sea bird had expired at my feet. The sight of dead animals, road kill, but especially birds, would forever elicit surges of melancholy and angst. The grief I felt had not a trace of spirituality. What I sensed was visceral, dark, menacing.

Many years later, as I went on assignment to Central America, the sight of dead birds would take on a new aura. Alive, birds symbolize freedom from earthly bounds. Dead, especially when placed on someone's doorstep, they telegraph a warning, the threat of a looming calamity. Several investigative reports I'd written had earned me ill-omened accolades: a dead pigeon whose unfurled wings had been stapled to a small funeral wreath and propped against my hotel room door at the Casa Grande in Guatemala City; two dead sparrows similarly positioned on the stoop of my rented studio in Copán. I'd somehow managed to keep one step ahead of my would-be assassins but I would never look at dead birds the same way again.

It was not surprising that the sight of the mutilated baby grackles, less than a week after I'd moved to Dranomos, would stir feelings of anxiety. I'd come down from the small cloud-shrouded mountain town of Patchahei to the high desert plateau where the sky is almost always blue and the sun percolates for months on end. Long, bitter snowy days and frigid nights at 4,000 feet had taken their toll and the prospect of gentler winters and warmer summers had beckoned me down from the summit. Little did I know.

Then, one day, I heard it: a whisper, a distant murmur; throaty at first then high-pitched as it subsided, like the sigh of a mortally wounded beast or the wail of a restless spirit. I couldn't tell where it was coming from. It ebbed and flowed like the tide, like an intermittent rustling of leaves. Like a draft squeezing through some narrow aperture.

A more thorough search for the source of these gloomy squalls took me to the laundry room, a small area with a door leading to the garage. To my relief, it was only the wind insinuating itself under the garage door and whistling with every gust.

I also thought I'd heard, merging with the reedy crescendo and ebbing of moans and whimpers, what sounded like laughter -- no, not the resonance of gaiety or merriment, not the giggle of children or the chortle of men telling salty jokes. What reached my ears, I thought, was a sequence of long sepulchral wails, otherworldly, warped by the newness of my circumstance in this austere, taciturn expanse of rock, sand, stunted Joshua trees, clumps of sagebrush and roving tumbleweed.

I'd spent the winter settling in, arraying the furniture, lining my favorite books on the shelves, placing bric-a-brac and curios on the mantelpiece and other outcroppings, adorning the walls with the pictures I'd painted and the lithographs I'd collected over the years. A happy loner too busy to be bored, I'd put off any interaction with my neighbors, few as they were, until spring. Now and then I'd spotted a couple of lonely figures dashing in and out of their houses, scurrying across my field of view as if they were being pursued by some menacing presence. It's not that I'd waited for the Welcome Wagon or a neighborly invitation to a family brunch. I could dispense with these niceties. I considered them pointless, synthetic and somewhat intrusive. It's just that I'd found it odd that my presence in this gated hamlet, this remote, desolate mesa ringed by barren, cratered hills had been largely unnoticed, if not ignored. So I'd happily gone back to work on what would perhaps be my magnum opus, my one-way ticket to the blue Mediterranean, the deliverance that penury and anonymity had so far denied me.

"We had our first snowfall," I wrote in my journal. Bad choice of a pronoun, I'd exclaimed. *We?* This is not an editorial position. I rewrote the sentence:

"It snowed last night. The mountain tops are peppered with white. A thick, ground-hugging fog is slowly chewing up the scenery. It's time for the Wellbutrin and a change in screensavers -- from the red and gold of a New England autumn to a sun-drenched islet set like an emerald on a turquoise sea and ringed with white sandy beaches and dotted with tall coconut trees swaying in the breeze. It's time to let my mind roam. It's time to hunker down, brave -- no, endure -- winter and watch for the first signs of spring.

I was what the gallant French refer to as *"entre deux âges,"* [middle-aged] and blunter Americans obliquely describe as "well past his prime": an old man who'd managed to ward off the ravages of time and the onset of decrepitude by keeping busy, stretching time.

Time is not a renewable resource. What cannot be prevented or changed must be weathered.

I'd always thought that every man has a "tale" locked up within him that, as it unfolds, struggles to emerge. "Every life is a best-seller." I'd come up with this aphorism when I lived in Queens,

New York on the 14th floor of a 16-story building. At night, across the playground, a building of equal stature revealed through dozens of lit windows a patchwork quilt of silent dramas, each circumscribed by time and space. The diminutive creatures in my field of view, I'd suddenly realized one evening, some unwinding in their living rooms, others readying for bed, others yet quarrelling or fixing dinner in closet-sized "galley" kitchens, each acting out a preordained scenario, must surely have a compelling story to tell that will never be told. I remembered feeling empathy for the strangers I spied upon in moments of introspection, each framed in his own shadow box, each engaged in life's mind-numbing, often absurd pantomime.

I'd learned a great deal about dignity and vulgarity, refinement and boorishness, solitude, boredom and carousing, and I'd realized that I too, at some time or other, must have been the object of someone's absent or amused scrutiny.

It had all happened so fast. I'd taken early retirement, left genteel Connecticut and set out on a five-day, 3,000-mile drive across America. Its vastness and awesome beauty had filled me with exhilaration and appeased for a while the emptiness within. The emptiness returned when I reached the desert. Behind me was the narrowing perspective of an arrow-straight road merging into the horizon line. Ahead lay a barren, petrified expanse. Alone in its vast, sallow bosom, overwhelmed by the immensity and desolation around me, I stopped, got out of the car and looked at the limitless blue vault above, dotted with strange cloud formations, some the shape of flying saucers, others wispy and elongated like lines of cocaine, others yet splaying like supernovas or metastasizing cells. I surveyed the tawny parched earth at my feet. Everywhere, clumps of sparse, stunted shrubs and contorted Joshua trees clung stubbornly to life in this lifeless citadel. I felt lost. I wanted to scream. The scream died in my throat as I set my eyes on a lone yellow poppy, its dainty orange petals quivering in the breeze. Memories cascaded through my mind. I remembered the wild blood-red poppy fields of Abu Gosh, outside Jerusalem, where I'd gamboled as a boy, taking in their heady aroma, napping under a blanket of undulating blood-red blossoms and dreaming Technicolor dreams. I remembered the wistful French love song of my youth, *"Comme un petit coquelicot,"* [Like a little poppy]. I'd been swept in a vortex of indescribable emotions every time I heard it. Poppies are still my favorite flowers. And I remembered Paris, the city of my birth. Words, images, colors and aromas danced inside my head, faint, disjointed, stranded at the limits of consciousness. I felt my tongue forming silent thoughts, like prayers or mantras. Emboldened by self-discovery, delivered from their cerebral bonds, the words gushed forth. It was a soliloquy of stupefying candor and sorrow, part confession, part supplication, words driven by longing, by despair, by a fear of madness, words one only dares to utter in the desert's deafening silence. I looked at the sky. Then I looked at the poppy and the babble ceased. It had wilted in my hand. But its subtle, intoxicating scent still lingered on the tip of my fingers, in my nose, on my lips.

"I should have never plucked it. I should have never set eyes upon it," I heard myself wailing as my eyes now strained against the milky glare of day.

Somewhere at the edge of a gray town, a cookie-cutter copy of a thousand gray tank towns, on a gray street senselessly named after some tree or flower, deep inside a gray room adorned with mementos and frozen glimpses of time misspent, the self-probing continues. I'm not in Paris or in New York but in a grim, far-flung gray tank town in the middle of nowhere. I'm out of range of the ultimate cause so I seek answers in the gray dancing shadows on the ceiling and hang on to rapidly dissolving shreds of graying memory.

America. Fifty-six years spent chasing after the same dream, lurching from a brief state of wonderment to one of frustration, disillusionment and anger as I stumbled on the desiccated fragments of discredited myths and embalmed fiction, trying to fit in, hopelessly out of step, out of tune. Yes, I'm a restive stranger, an untamed renegade, ill at ease in my own skin, an interloper in a realm I do not fully fit in, outwardly housebroken, inwardly raging and defiant and aching, treading unfamiliar waters, lost in the blinding light of day. Fifty-six years: Two billion heartbeats pumping life into an out-of-soul experience, each pulse adding to my estrangement and perplexity.

The poppies are now in bloom. I scan the high desert mountains that surround me, dwarf me, fence me in and deny me the privilege of a horizon line where freedom looms.

Somewhere in the distance, a car rumbles by like a great booming wall of sound.

In Dranomos, I'd quickly learned, neighbors had no tales to tell. Ghostly, furtive, aloof, poker-faced, they seemed to live like me -- hermits in a wasteland of topographic banality and cultural sterility, un-ordained monks who live in self-created cloisters where time, frigid winters and long periods of lung-searing heat and drought mummify the body and scorch the soul.

It would be a while before the doves began cooing at the advent of spring but by then I knew that the wind, the heat, the unbearable sameness of it all had rendered everyone insane and that I would escape a similar fate only by fleeing from this morose, howling desert. What I hadn't reckoned yet was whether I'd make my getaway trussed in a straightjacket, screaming as the wind added its voice to the sinister chorus of evil laughter, or carted away on a gurney inside a body bag.

Last week two lizards and two field mice drowned in the pool.

Yesterday, I retrieved a dead bat.

On cloudless days, as the sun begins its slow westward descent, an inscription -- a name -- materializes, as if fashioned by some spectral hand, at the bottom of the pool. It reads HILLARY AN. I would later learn that Hillary An, a former tenant, had drowned in the pool. Some say it was suicide. The wind, they surmise, had driven her mad.

Early this morning, my old friend Guy died of leukemia. He was cremated and his ashes were scattered, as he had instructed, from the top of a mountain where eagles nest. Guy thought birds are the reincarnated souls of men freed from their earthly shackles.

I turn my gaze heavenward at a searing, implacable sun. Then I look at my shoes, caked with brown desert dust. I remember the damp slippery clay by my mother's grave.

TIME FLIES

*Time is what hinders everything from
being given all at once.*
Henry Bergson

It began with a premise, a subtle hypothesis of stunning magnitude: When positive and negative gravitational forces are set on a collision course at retrograde absolute speed, the theory asserts, the impact creates a void inside which time can be frozen -- life extended, you hear -- perhaps forever.

So the Foundation approved the grant and a team of biophysicists and geneticists from the Theoretical Physics Research Institute and two eager *Drosophila melanogaster*, or fruit flies -- a male and a female -- went to work to test this astonishing concept.

The flies were placed in a biotronic accelerator, a state-of-the-art synchrotron developed by the Institute's Entomo-Ontological Laboratory.

Temperature constants and reverse wavelength spectral illumination were maintained throughout the project.

Three seconds later, the fruit flies mated with great eagerness. The first pupae hatched forty seconds later.

On the fourth day, or three hundred thousand fruit-fly generations later, fifteen offspring matured and exceeded their natural life expectancy by twelve hours, the equivalent of four human years.

Early on the twelfth night, sixty-six flies outlived their earliest progenitors by five hundred and eighteen fly-years.

A male and a female were removed from the accelerator and released outdoors on the seventeenth day. Six thousand fly-years had elapsed and all memory of an earlier life, of a once uncontrolled and free existence, had since been erased.

Disoriented, dazed by the sudden foreboding vastness around them, the flies climbed erratically toward the limitless expanse. Feeling the sun's breath upon their wings, aroused by some anomalous threat, they flew toward each other, met and clasped briefly in mid-air before imploding and vanishing without a trace.

The rest, having lived six million years in human-equivalent age, were destroyed on the twenty-first day with massive isotopic concentrations. Their potential life span can only be expressed in astronomical terms.

Immortality? Easy. It's all neatly packaged in a self-nullifying theorem. Georg Wilhelm Friedrich Hegel would have been proud. But involuntary confinement and loss of selfhood is a high price to pay for immortality.

And so, Project Fruit Fly was scrubbed. The Institute issued a carefully worded summary report that no one bothered to read and which was subsequently consigned to a dark and dusty vault at the National Archives.

Invoking the Freedom of Information Act, I requested a copy. The request was denied, first on "administrative grounds," then for reasons of "national security." I appealed. The appeal was rejected. I was cautioned not to insist. The warning had the bureaucratic incivility accorded a pesky nobody or a dangerous agitator.

And then one day, not far in the future, the few who could afford their own biotronic accelerator granted themselves life eternal; the many who could not, lived and died serving them.

One Night in Copán

DEATH & TRANSFIGURATION

*You can't be free to become what you want when you're
starving, sorely oppressed or stunted in your moral growth
by a life of endless drudgery [in a society] where the free development
of the few is bought at the cost of the shackling of the many.*
Terry Eagleton

Across town, two derelicts identified by police as Floyd
Horton, 39, and Cecil Glenville, 42, froze to death
overnight in their dreams. They were found huddled on a bench
at Dag Hammarskjold Plaza, on East 47th Street, a stone's-throw
away from the United Nations building. They'd wrapped
themselves in newsprint and plastic sheeting to ward off the
cold but New York's bitter winter night claimed them just the
same. Their bodies had stiffened and turned blue when they
were carted away.

Horton's remains were cremated free of charge by the City.
His ashes, as are those unclaimed by family or friend, now
fatten the soil at an upstate experimental horticultural farm.

Glenville, who had a cousin in Connecticut, was buried in a

pine box with a plain metal marker at the local potter's field.

A week later, requesting anonymity, Glenville's cousin had the body exhumed for reburial at the family crypt in Darien. When the coffin was unsealed, Glenville was found lying face down, his knuckles caked with blood, his fingernails torn off. His eyes were wide open, his mouth agape in silent horror. A crimson crust coated his nostrils and lips.

Cryogenics Unlimited, the outfit that keeps utopians on ice until the elusive Lazarus Factor is synthesized, was called in to inspect Glenville's remains. Hard at work on the development of an enzyme that offers the dead another lease on life, technicians at Cryogenics Unlimited theorized that Glenville had somehow thawed and slowly stirred back to consciousness like a hibernating toad.

"Realizing he'd been entombed alive, [Glencille] must have suffered a massive heart attack," read the coroner's report. Glenville was cremated and not even the Lazarus Factor can help him now.

Floyd Horton, his misery reduced to phosphate-rich sublimates, endows long-stem pink roses with a very special blush.

PAST IMPERFECT

Not to be born surpasses thought and speech.
The second best is to have seen the light
and then gone back quickly whence we came.
Sophocles

If the latest theoretical physics fad has any merit, a moment recorded in time, it purports, is a moment exhausted. What this axiom suggests is that impermanence is reality's only constant. Only what remains *uncreated* escapes the shift from potentiality to actuality, from imminence to nothingness. To *be*, for all intents and purposes, is prelude to the unavoidable end of being.

For "Otto," betrayed by the laws of probability, mocked by fate and spurned by his maker, *being* was unavoidably the essence of his finality. Unloved, deprived of a memory and short on dreams, Otto, poor Otto, is no sooner conjured from the dregs of an ancient genesis than undone, nullified and jettisoned into the abyss of oblivion. Were it not for some insightful and long-since forgotten astropaleobiologist, his living nightmare --

set at the beginning of time -- might never have been chronicled.

Unschooled and tentative, tolerated but never tamed, nature turned its back on itself and sanctioned -- some say, "with a vengeance" -- the spontaneous advent of a bizarre and unique life form. Ponder, if you can, an organism so vile, so grotesque, so pathetic in countenance, so tortured and twisted, and so utterly purposeless that it lived less than one Earth spin around its axis. Otto's sudden emergence and abrupt demise defies the canons of evolution; it has no antecedent, it fits no known paradigm. The very laws of thermodynamics are being upended in the process. Serenely unconcerned, entropy spares the miserable "thing" the passage of time. It is an unlikely act of compassion in a realm of cosmic unconcern.

Discovered in meteoric debris, Otto's fossilized remains reveal a brutish organism, apparently legless but equipped with a prehensile tail with which it flogged itself and copulated through an orifice doubling as its mouth. Paleontologists agreed that the improbable entity was covered with a scaly, mottled hide, and that its single eye, capable of polychromatic sight, was probably endowed with a gentle, almost seductive expression. Otto is also credited to have been capable of emitting piercing moans so rueful that they all but froze the hearts of those who may have heard it. The Grand Lexicon of Random Biogenic Anomalies confirms the existence of cosmic influences capable of inducing *auto*-asexual reproduction, though none quite as peculiar as Otto -- as the monstrosity was christened.

The ancestor and sole offspring -- the auto-progeny -- of a freak process that doomed it to genetic irrelevance, Otto is believed to have succumbed from exhaustion brought on by futile attempts to reproduce. Tritium dating has tentatively placed the appearance and virtually simultaneous disappearance of this as yet unclassified phenomenon at 500 trillion year ago.

Otto's remains were laid to rest and a monument was erected to commemorate the momentous find and incongruity.

Signs of Man, the legendary if hypothetical vertebrate believed to have accidentally emerged at an earlier period, are never found. An acceptable theory justifying his advent and arguing his brief and noxious tenancy on a minor planet in the Milky Way Galaxy has not yet been postulated. None is forthcoming.

IN HIS OWN IMAGE

There is no absolute, no reason,
no God, no spirit at work in the world: nothing
but the brute instinctive will to live.
Arthur Schopenhauer

It had never been done. It would never be tried again. Not even in a dream. Here was an unrepeatable chance event that upended the laws of potentiality and defied the very core of reason. Bear with me. Imagine absurdity challenging the sublime. Picture the unthinkable. And yet, against all odds, preposterous as it sounds, it happened: A driving force, heretofore unimagined, the offspring of a staggering abstraction that can't be annulled once spawned -- nor left unexplored -- burst out of a single, indissoluble vanishing point.

Reaching into nonexistence (or emerging from it?) now ponderable if not fully manifest, suspended somewhere between immanence and dizzying inscrutability (as are all things when first caused), he endowed himself with being. In a single surge of cognition, exceeding his creative potential, he was now his own *fait accompli*. He had just invented himself.

Free from his cerebral cocoon, fully transfigured from genderless ambiguity to virile causality, he surveyed his completeness. Heeding a time scale of his own calibration, anxious to add purpose to will, meaning to intent, momentum to stimulus, he separated cause from effect, quintessence from character, provenance from possibility, state from circumstance, identity from distinction, metaphor from divergence. In short, he elaborated all manner of paradox and contrariety which would forever set him apart from those who are not, and can never be *him*.

To avert any confusion between him and the teeming realm his incarnation would evoke, he relinquished form for unquantifiable symmetry; he traded transparency for impenetrability. His geometry would be indivisible and without limit, here brimming with presence, there immersed in desolation so vast that even time would stand still at points unmarked and of his own design.

He then granted himself the capacity to remain unmoved by sorrow and calamity. To justify such dispassion, he endowed himself with ostensible kindness and discernible unkindness, allowing himself to be perceived as possessing equal amounts of benevolence and evil, munificence and heartlessness, genius and imbecility, as circumstance dictated, and depending upon prevailing moods and attitudes.

Now armed with an ego, he gave himself an indecipherable name by which others would know him. Some followed him in silent awe. Others, whose cries were never heard, wept and suffered and died forgotten because pain, by some outlandish precept, is a path out of bondage. His ear inattentive and his breast unfaithful to the throngs who called on him and sought his succor, he was forgotten, in time, like a distant tragedy, like a bad dream.

Cynics suggested that he'd been a figment of his own imagination. Others, with greater forbearance, offered that, in a supreme act of mercy, having lost faith in his own inflated image, using his extraordinary powers, he nullified himself for the good of all.

A great, raging, thunderous roar shook his domain. And the legend, so carefully preserved and perpetuated, was soon forgotten. No one knows for sure whether he was insane or whether those he caught in his devilish trap had lost all reason.

And peace eternal reigned at last upon the remnant few left to ponder the incongruity of being God.

THE LONGEST NIGHT

Deep into that darkness peering, long I stood there,
wondering, fearing, doubting, dreaming dreams
no mortal ever dared to dream before.
Edgar Allan Poe

Smokers rebel. Segregated, sneered and coughed at -- "ours is an unreasoned, even absurd pleasure," they fume, "but it shall not be abrogated."

"Smokers may well have the right to smoke," nonsmokers retort, "but that entitlement deprives us of our right not to inhale their foul exhalations."

Intoxicated by their own emissions, if not by their disregard for the well-being of others, smokers reject their nemeses' argument as "capricious and arbitrary." Citing the Preamble to the Declaration of Independence which, they insist, endows them with certain inalienable rights, they counter that smoking is a form of free speech protected by the First Amendment to the Constitution.

Sensing free publicity, the Environmental Protection Agency

promptly sides with nonsmokers in hopes of diverting attention from its own hazy record.

Arguing that the *smoker vs. nonsmoker* issue is constitutionally insoluble, the Supreme Court recesses for an afternoon nap.

Smokers keep puffing in designated areas where it is still tolerated, thanks to civil libertarians who would gladly lay down their own lives to protect a smoker's right to die of heart disease, emphysema or lung cancer. Evenhandedness often leads to absurdity.

Fights erupt. Spontaneous demonstrations turn out ugly crowds in cities around the world, all barking savage insults and threats.

In the City of Brotherly Love an angry roar rises from the mob. All heads turn in unison toward the third-floor landing of a once-elegant townhouse. At the end of a rope suspended from a flagpole flying Old Glory, bound together like ham-hocks, dangle the cadavers of a man and a woman caught smoking in defiance of an ordinance prohibiting such activity within city limits. Stirred no doubt by feelings of altruism, anti-smoking vigilantes had rammed a fistful of cigarettes down their throats.

A few bury their faces, horrified or overcome with shame. Others flee the ghastly scene, vomiting in their tracks. The rest, their qualms flaking away like dead bits of conscience, keep looking in mute fascination.

Wholesale persecution soon follows.

In Los Angeles, the police purge smokers from their ranks and transfer them to the sanitation corps. Most adjust quite well once they discover the metaphysical connection between police work and garbage.

The earth sizzles with rage. The world goes amok.

In Washington, several legislators who at long last concede that smoking is a deadly addiction countenanced by other legislators because it generates huge taxable revenues -- introduce stiff anti-smoking bills. Others, who refuse to return certain favors graciously extended by the tobacco lobby, are slain.

Tobacco companies respond by making falsehearted anti-smoking pronouncements on television and radio, and in print publications. *"Smoking is addictive and dangerous to your health,"* their ads proclaim. What is left unsaid is that their factories continue to produce millions of cigarettes -- just in case. Their domestic profits slowly turning to ashes, the tobacco companies now rot the unregulated lungs of the Third World.

Counting more smokers per capita than all other nations combined, Japan and China are decimated. The once-buzzing squadrons of polite bespectacled little chain-smoking shutterbugs wearing awkward little western suits have since gone home and now engage in the gentler pursuit of writing three-line poems, dwarfing trees and carving cricket cages out of matchsticks.

Gays and lesbians are next. The deaf; the color-blind; the morbidly obese; the elderly; the miscegenated. The widowed are summarily executed. Redheads undergo mass sterilization. The albino and the flatfooted perish in a bonfire of condescension. Forced to read Chaucer, dyslexics die a horrible death. Stamp collectors are canceled.

There is no shortage of latent martyrs. Others will surely be found.

Soon, one last wisp of smoke rises from the embers like a pipe dream and scatters in the air for the last time.

I blow out the candle. It will be a long night.

NEITHER APE NOR ANGEL

Which is it? Is man God's only mistake
or God man's only mistake?
Friedrich Wilhelm Nietzsche

Every now and then, usually by default and seldom on the first try, the human race blunders on a fact or two. Wrenched from the shadows of ignorance or simply sideswiped by some careless time traveler, these truths often shatter deep-seated if somewhat unsustainable beliefs.

Take Homo sapiens, for example.

In the beginning, when fate still ruled the world, when providence, not scheme, random chance, not purpose or plan molded man's destiny, two camps vied for the truth; and both held it for a while.

Fat and sated like iguanas basking in the sun, wading in and out of the primordial soup where it's cozy and warm, Darwinists made no bones about it. Their blueprint was sound. Evolution made sense. One by one, the pieces of the gigantic puzzle began to fit into place with such symmetry as to make some transcendental first cause -- divine or other -- not only quite probable but essential. They just didn't call it God.

Angered by Darwin's seeming irreverence, outraged by the notion that they might be descended from apes, not angels, Creationists kept invoking divine intervention, as though evolution were not in itself a wondrous phenomenon. And life went on.

One day, for no apparent reason, and as if there was an urgent need to know, cosmologists everywhere began splitting cosmic hair. With the Big Bang versus the Steady State debate well behind them, though still deadlocked on several core issues, they now asked each other (and themselves, no doubt): is the universe "open" or "closed?" Does intergalactic space extend indefinitely and in all directions, or do as yet undetected boundaries found only at some inscrutably distant point mark its final limits? If so, what lies beyond? What is *space,* anyway, they asked. Is it a circumstantial realm with no intrinsic dimension, no reality of its own except that which is fancied by man in his convoluted ruminations? Is *space* a byproduct of human consciousness, like *time,* which is seen as "passing" but in fact does not move? Some insisted that space is not only endowed with quantifiable form and volume, but that it is also measurable by a timeline that includes a starting point, a first cause, or alpha, but not necessarily an omega. Others retorted with disarming logic that something that has no boundaries cannot possibly have shape.

Surely, while these mental pirouettes severely strained the limits of awareness, others yet agreed that the issue was the sphere of philosophy and mysticism. After all, probes sent out on scouting missions to the farthest reaches of the inky void had gone on one-way odysseys and no one knew for sure what they would run into, or when.

For a while, the case for an open (or infinite) universe gained ground. Infinity is a tolerable abstraction because, like all absolutes, it is as self-limiting as it is unquantifiable. Something that has no shape or computable dimensions, however keenly one may try to comprehend it, has no being. Sometimes ignorance is bliss, even among the learned.

In time, however, unable to bolster their respective positions, cosmologists reached an impasse -- and a compromise. It became fashionable to argue that, for lack of a more convincing explanation, perpetual space-time and cosmic confinement may be one and the same. The choice, they offered, lay in the mind's eye of poets and stargazers and dreamers and a science fiction writer or two. It was, pardon the irresistible witticism, pretty much an open and shut case. Adding to the confusion, perhaps out of desperation, perhaps in an attempt to blur the distinction between knowledge and whimsy, someone suggested that reality is a hologram. Someone else theorized that the universe has no reality except in God's boundless imagination. And another millennium came and went in a cosmos unconcerned with the pitiable struggles and contests of a wretched organism that keeps breeding itself out of existence.

And then it happened, not unexpectedly perhaps, but with devastating finality.

"WE ARE ALONE!" banner headlines proclaimed. **"HUMANKIND: AN ACCIDENT"** they screamed impiously on all the front pages.

Carefully worded, unadorned, brutally prosaic, eloquently detached, spreading across the page, the article ignited passions, provoked outrage or apoplectic stupor, clouded the mind, froze the spirit.

"An international team of astrophysicists has released details of a study which confirms that 'intelligent life' is confined to planet Earth, and that the odds of a similar biogenic manifestation occurring elsewhere in the universe are close to

nil.

"*Dismissing critics who charge that such view smacks of 'cosmic egocentricity,' the study recommends that the search for extraterrestrial life be halted and that efforts and assets be refocused on heretofore neglected earthbound priorities such as overpopulation, climate change, poverty, hunger, disease and diminishing natural resources.*

"*Drafted by the Yearly Astrophysical Hagiographic Watch Experiment in Hyperspace (YAHWEH), the 2,000-page document asserts that, 'life is the aftermath of a spontaneous and unrepeatable paradox,' and that humankind, is 'an experiment gone wrong.'*

"*Alluding to Albert Einstein's celebrated rebuff, 'God does not play dice with the universe,' a spokesman for YAHWEH said that 'God had indeed played dice with the universe and lost. Perched atop a speck of dust in the limitless void,' the study concluded, 'aided by providence and propelled by natural selection, the human race is an occurrence -- an accident -- the result of an endless succession of unpremeditated chance events, all of which continue to unfold as we travel through time, as the present conjugates itself forever and ever and ever.'*

"*Supporting YAHWEH's conclusions, a joint communiqué issued by the world's spiritual leaders upheld the scientific findings. In an extraordinary gesture of humility and conciliation, quoting Boethius -- 'As far as you are able, join faith to reason' -- the communiqué conceded that 'God, the epitome of perfection,' had let his imagination run wild when He fashioned humans, and that unlike humans who never seem to learn from past mistakes, 'He had then been mindful not to repeat such abomination elsewhere in His dominion.'"*

From that moment on, and for the first time since the dawning of the age of reality, everyone knew that God would never be reached for comment, no matter how hard one tried. And in classrooms all across the land, children learned about the Punic Wars and the square of the hypotenuse and Charlemagne and the mighty Ganges and about life in a drop of pond water. The children grew up and ego devoured the innocence of youth. In time, apes became extinct and man vanished soon after from the face of the earth. Only angels survived the merciful finale; angels, little green Martians, the Loch Ness monster, Big Foot, the Abominable Snowman, Sasquatch, the Chupacabra and all the other creatures that populate our dreams.

One Night in Copán

DREAMFARER

We Earth Men have a talent for ruining big, beautiful things.
The only reason we didn't set up hot-dog stands
in the midst of the Egyptian temple of Karnak
is because it was out of the way
and served no large commercial purpose.
Ray Bradbury, The Martian Chronicles

You must've heard. Touchdown took place early this morning on a desolate stretch of the Tharsis Bulge in the shadows of cloud-ringed Mount Olympus. Violent squalls of swirling carbon dioxide had delayed final descent. It took all of my piloting skills and the capsule's exceptional maneuverability to help maintain the right downward thrust-to-weight ratio for a near-perfect landing.

Bent by gravity, distorted by cosmic rays and electromagnetic waves, sounds of euphoria, distant, almost alien, soon began to crackle on the radio. It was Mission Control. I heard the thunderous applause of a thousand jubilant specialists. Bone-tired and listless, I acknowledged Earth perhaps more tersely than I'd intended. I asked for everyone's indulgence, turned off the transmitter and surrendered to sleep.

A frozen silence now fills my ears. I'm peering beyond the pockmarked spaceport, through rising gales of pelting sand and dust. Before me, stretches a crumpled terrain the color of anger. Its disfigured visage splits into winding trenches that look like dry riverbeds. Here and there, jagged nickel-iron meteorites protrude from the sandy surface. Water, if it ever existed, has either long since evaporated or is now permanently frozen deep beneath the surface. I'll know soon enough. To the east, the sky is a rich brassy copper. Farther north it assumes a ruddy hue. Another storm is fast approaching. Brooding, it will erupt with untold fury as invisible demons claw at the tortured landscape and obscure it from view.

What I see of Mars through the porthole, and what I will face tomorrow as I alight on the planet's surface will best be told in pictures. Cameras have no soul, only eyes. That's what keeps them honest. They will record the awesome spectacle with poetic unconcern.

What I feel is less easily defined, far more prone to understatement or exaggeration. Feelings, like dreams, are hard to apprehend and just as slippery. I shall not risk distorting them by analyzing them just yet; perhaps when I return to Earth; *if* I return to Earth. This is Mars, I keep telling myself, the fourth planet from the Sun, an old friend now at last chanced upon face to face.

Sunrise: my first on Mars. Will it be my last? Remote, aloof, no bigger than the moonlit eye of a prairie wolf, the sun sets Olympus Mons' barren ridges afire, sending a kaleidoscopic scattering of ochre, burnt umber and blood-red into the thin golden sky. Wispy contrails of ice crystals levitate against the forbidding blackness of space. How very strange for a dead planet to be enshrined in vestments of such daunting beauty.

I shut my eyes but a star-studded canopy spreads out against my closed eyelids. This is Mars or else I must be dreaming. Only in a dream can the folly, the arrogance, the deceptive face of reality seem so vivid. Mars? I may as well have journeyed to Venus or mighty Jupiter or enigmatic Saturn or self-effacing Pluto, or some other celestial neighborhood, undiscovered, unsuspected, barely imagined, not unlike the unexplored regions of the psyche, perhaps even like this dream.

Forgive the metaphors, the circuitous twists of thought, the gloomy sophistry of it all. I, who always took pride in the clarity of my reasoning power, I now drown in a vortex of sensations forever crippled by the meagerness of words. How do I paint a point in space? How do I behold the face of God? By surrendering to sightless, speechless slumber? Perchance by dreaming? After all a dream is a voyage to the end of night. But unlike a cruise or the clan's yearly motorcade to Aunt Bertha's clambake a dream has no fixed itinerary, no scheduled destination. It just unfolds. And there's no need to pack.

It is the very nature of such journeys that compels those of us who embark on their gossamer wings to question their significance or merit. What's the point? Why wander when the old armchair cradles our weary frames and conformity extends its all-embracing arms the better to receive us? We are apt to discover on arrival at some unscheduled port of call, as I did on Mars' barren shores, that there may have been no good reason to make the trek in the first place. For when all is said and done, at the very end of some aimless expedition, worn out and confused, we will sadly conclude that some dreams are just too close for comfort, some dreams are just not meant to be.

So I wake up.

Opalescent moonbeams filter through my bedroom's lace curtains and I see shadows dancing on the wall. Could dawn be far behind? On the short ride to the launch pad, past Building D where tomorrow's dreamers train, I'm struck by the notion that knowledge is rewarded with an ever-widening chasm of ignorance and superstition.

Today is the first day of winter -- December 21, 2012. The sun is aligned with the plane of our galaxy. At its center, the gigantic black hole is as black and elusive as ever. Earth's magnetic field has not changed. The only calamities recorded on this fateful date echo man's bestial cruelty to man. Apocalypse has been big business for 2,000 years or more. From ancient Persia to Daniel and Enoch and Habakkuk and Ezekiel and the deranged author of Revelation and the death-obsessed Maya, deceivers and impostors and self-deluded mystics acting under the pretense of divine inspiration have hoodwinked the multitudes and driven them to act like lunatics.

As I ease myself into the pilot's seat, I tell myself that future explorers, however vast their knowledge might be, will bear burdens of ignorance immensely heavier than my own. But once aloft, their sails will hug the wind and ride the tempest. For, they too shall have dared to go beyond their dreams as prophets of doom, foiled again, rewrite their contemptible scripts.

THE VAMPIRE STATE *

Like flies to wanton boys, are we to the gods.
They kill us for their sport.
William Shakespeare -- *King Lear*

A rank, sulfurous halo hangs low over Manhattan. Driven by icy gusts, tentacle-like fingers of swirling amber gases swoop toward the slime-slick pavement, probing deep into yawning doorways, arcades and atria, seeking out the specters that lurk within their drafty expanse.

It's Christmas Eve in the Big Apple. Chiming in the distance in pious unison, ethereal and uninvolved, church bells summon the faithful. Chiming? No, *tolling* -- a lugubrious knell for a swarming, moribund metropolis, for the one thousand and one night creatures that stalk its streets, for the living dead I get paid to hunt down and kill.

It all came together half a century ago or more when politicians,

---

* *First published in the December 1991 issue of OMNI Magazine.*

anxious to save face and give voters the impression that justice was being served, let the long simmering rancor, the restive hatred burst like an ugly abscess. Violence, sporadic and extemporaneous at first, grew bolder and deadlier with each secret municipal emergency meeting.

No one complained. Not a single cry of horror was ever heard. It was too late. Justice -- like truth -- the stronger of two conflicting arguments, justice, the paradox suspended on the tip of a sword, put on its most fearsome face. The Lady took off the blindfold and winked lasciviously at the oligarchs. And the carnage began.

'Tis the season of all folly, falalalala ... and the blood of the young, thinner than water, cheaper than hogwash, coalesces with the putrid rivulets of swill and excrement that hug the curb and cascade into the storm drains.

Torn by crime, soaring unemployment, triple-digit inflation, homelessness, merciless slashes in social services, suffocated by Orwellian federal statutes, America's big cities are putrefying and crumbling like the toes of a leper. For every child who wakes up poor and hungry, another dies of neglect or abuse. One-parent families are now the norm, each producing its quota of junkies and juvenile offenders. America has the world's largest and fastest growing prison population. More than four million minors are in custody on charges ranging from truancy and drug use to petty theft and prostitution. Two million more serve hard time for capital crimes: murder, rape, aggravated assault, armed robbery and home invasion. Most are incarcerated with hardened adult criminals -- ten to a cell. There is no more room.

As the chasm between rich and poor widens, a larger number of affluent urban dwellers move out to escape the squalor, the skyrocketing city taxes, the violence and the decaying infrastructure. The exodus turns cities and towns into tracts of depravity, disease and social unrest.

Sparked by a growing demand for slave labor and conscripts, immigration from the Third World keeps adding to the ranks of the poor, the marginally educated and the culturally estranged segments of society. Many future felons start out as street children. Most of the minors who live on the streets and in the catacombs and sewers beneath subway and railroad tunnels suffer from mental disorders. Drug-induced dementia and a form of premature Parkinsonism blamed on raging air and water pollution, afflict thousands of others. Thousands more have perished at the hands of vigilantes, sexual psychopaths and agents of the state, all meting out their brand of justice. There are simply too many kids out there.

Inexplicably, in one last spasm of puritanical fervor, bolstered by an apostate Supreme Court and a Church obsessed with the unborn but indifferent to the living, "pro-lifers" at last succeed in reversing *Roe vs. Wade* and in making abortion a federal crime punishable by death. The oligarchs must be assured a steady supply of cheap labor; the Church a steady supply of dues-paying penitents.

I get paid to pluck the fruits of this incestuous union.

It's eleven forty. Byron is thirteen, resourceful, clever. I've shadowed him day and night for nearly a month, clambering up and down the byways and alleyways he and his cronies scour in search of shelter or easy prey -- old folks or stragglers stranded in the night.

Midnight. Christmas is greeted with spontaneous acts of vandalism and drunken displays of nudity. There is little cheer. Off of Eighth Avenue, behind the Port Authority Bus Terminal's mazelike network of ramps and underpasses, a band of nine-

and ten-year-olds take turns scrounging through trash bins and peeking through the windows of a dingy motel where couples come to risk procreation in exchange for the shallow reward of a brief grunt of pleasure. A block away, a pedophile barters with a twelve-year-old. Envious and resentful, four urchins encircle and pounce on their competition.

It's now two fifty a.m. Alone, leaning against a pile of cardboard boxes by the wharf, near the old Fulton Fish Market, Byron is hallucinating. It could be glue or crack or the new rage in town -- stalactites -- a deadly mix of acetone-imbibed cannabis, rubber cement and denatured alcohol. Byron is armed and dangerous.

Byron spots me. He freezes. I unsheathe my revolver and point it at him, slowly, confidently, with the panache granted men whose conscience is stilled by the exigencies of job and duty. Byron spreads his arms, Christ like, and rests his head against his shoulder. He smiles. Defiance, stoicism, relief are all etched in his life-hardened baby face, in those glassy eyes where night's eerie scintillations shimmer. He looks at me without rancor, a martyr without a cause, a sacrificial lamb whose sacrifice brings about no redemption. I squeeze the trigger, repeatedly, remorselessly, thankful that another street child, alone and hungry since birth, abused and abandoned by his family, mistreated by his peers, another boy nobody smiles at, nobody cuddles, nobody protects, nobody comforts, nobody loves, will never again sully the society that begat him.

Childhood is when the future begins. Death is when memories expire. Byron never had a future. I revoked his past. It's a living. I must not philosophize. I obey orders. The cost of a family Christmas dinner keeps going up. Thank God I get overtime.

(From the secret diaries of Lt. Joe Krolick, NYPD, December 24-25, in the Year of Our Lord, 2062).

A HARVEST OF SORROWS

Evolution follows a path of descent and thus
provides the world with a basis for pessimism.
Anonymous

Getting lost in a place Jeremiah hardly knew was not on the program that day. Out of prudence more than inclination, he followed one of the main arteries, a long, wide street paved with cobblestones, flanked on each side by willows whose branches met midpoint above it to form a shady dome of green and extending, as far as he could tell, to the horizon line.

Jeremiah kept walking, passing row after row of multiple-occupancy dwellings each set on a cul-de-sac on either side of the road, some flying oversized flags, others proclaiming their faith with tawdry displays of holy statuary and sacred icons on porches and lawns, others yet professing their love of God and country by warning intruders that their homes were fortified with all manner of automatic ordnance.

Rising in the distance, faint at first, clearer as he continued toward it, a massive billboard straddled the roadway. It read:

YOUR ARE ENTERING GEHENNA
PROCEED AT OWN PERIL

The road ended abruptly in rubbles of shattered rock and splintered cobbles a foot or so past the sign. Beyond it a yawning incline ended in a sheer drop. Extending from the base of a deep abyss, a steamy chasm stretched below as far as the eye could see.

Gehenna's unimaginable Stygian depths spilled open before Jeremiah like a lanced boil. Spanning an arroyo through which flows, like pus, a malodorous rivulet of greenish-colored swill, an old bridge heavy with traffic and swarming with street vendors separates a would-be purgatory from the pestilential netherworld below.

Reaching the base of the bridge was no easy task. Jeremiah followed a dizzying spiral of steep ascents and lateral downward convolutions, first through a darkened arcade reeking of urine where a teenage couple copulated against a wall, then down a fetid stairwell where rats, oblivious to it all, fed from a pile of fast-food containers, and, finally, around ditches and embankments covered knee-high with rotting refuse.

Escher's impossible architectures came to mind; then Kafka's schizoid plots; then Hieronymus Bosch's diabolic renderings of reality. And when Jeremiah alit under the arch, perspiring and out of breath, he knew he'd set foot on some spectral domain where outcasts and wastrels, the spurned and the unloved congregate like ghosts doomed to roam the void.

On the long and narrow ledge that hugs the foot of the bridge lives a family of seven, perhaps more. Rawboned, spidery, disheveled, prematurely old, a woman folds and refolds, sorts and rearranges a precious few possessions with a tedium induced by boredom or despair or madness. There's a pile of soiled rags for bedding, plastic bags to shield against the rain, a metal box to keep the tinder dry, a pot, scorched, misshapen and swarming with vermin, a disemboweled foam-rubber cushion to lean against on starry nights, a frayed straw hat, a sooty, half-burned candle, and a rumpled picture of a blond, blue-eyed, pink-faced Christ smiling quizzically at the world. Tugging at a fleshless, sagging teat, an infant squirms and whimpers with frustration.

The woman bares a toothless grin. Sitting on his heels, a man -- her husband? -- is busy pounding back into shape an unyielding slab of iron with a wooden mallet. The metal will not give but he keeps on striking it time after time with an obstinacy that bears little fruit. There is no emotion on the man's waxen face, not a trace of impatience or anticipation or annoyance at the futility of his Sisyphean ordeal. Staring into space, visibly exhausted but unwilling to quit, he persists, lost in a hypnotic syncopation that marks the passage of time.

Below, perched on an earthen mound overgrown with weeds, two toddlers, both flaunting distended bellies and herniated navels, rummage for worms. Barefoot, naked, soiled, green slime oozing from their nostrils, oblivious to the horror that surrounds them, they shriek with delight with every worm they pluck from the sludge. A few feet away, a young girl squats and relieves herself. A youngster, perhaps her brother, barely older and small for his age, sleeps nearby; one arm folded over his eyes to block out the light, the other extended and limp. Clasped in his hand is a small can of cobbler's glue. He risks not waking up. Oblivion is a one-way trip. Sniffing glue is a dead-end occupation; literally.

"Hey, you!" Jeremiah calls out. Startled, the boy stirs from a dark, dreamless slumber. His eyes don't open fully but he reflexively tightens a childlike grip around the small can of glue.

Turning on his side, compressing himself into a fetal position then stretching like a cat rousing from a nap, he makes contact with reality. Jeremiah places a reassuring hand on the boy's shoulder.

The boy staggers to a sitting position, rubs eyes thick with stupefaction and insensibility, and grants Jeremiah a lifeless, clammy handshake. An odious smell of uncleanness fills the air, soon neutralized by the pungent odor of glue on his breath.

"Where am I? Who are you," asks Jeremiah. The boy uncaps the can of toluene-based rubber cement, passes the opening over his nose and mouth, and inhales deeply, avidly. Jeremiah looks at him, detecting subtle signs of aphasia. Averting his eyes, the boy answers in monosyllables, seeking to save face in ambiguity and equivocation. But such ruse could well denote the presence of a host of other latent syndromes, all resulting from the corrosive effects of inhalants on the cerebral cortex.

"Where am I? Who are you," Jeremiah repeats. Attempting a smile, the boy scratches a lice-infested head, and draws another long snort of glue.

"Where are you?" The boy chuckles dejectedly "You're in my world of darkness, in this accursed valley. *Who am I,"* he echoes, his inflection tinted with grim solemnity and bitterness, his voice raspy and sepulchral. Sniffing glue devours sinuses and lungs. It produces horrible hallucinations. Irreversible brain damage and kidney failure are never far behind. Such fate seldom deters those who, like this boy, seem to fear life more than death.

The woman on the ledge unleashes a barrage of invectives at the boy. Jeremiah has trouble understanding the words but her tone and gestures convey impatience, disgust. The boy dismisses her with a wave of the hand.

"Screw you, you're not my mother," he mutters, with more than a trace of envy and sadness. Jeremiah and the boy shake hands again, this time in a complex ritual involving palm-smacking and finger-twisting. The boy takes leave, a longing smile on his lips, and ambles toward the water's edge where other kids are busy sniffing glue as the river's putrid current travels its lazy course.

"Who am I!" he yells out, this time in the exclamatory. "You tell me, mister." He laughs a raucous laugh, more like a bark. "Yes, mister, you tell me."

The woman plugs away at her senseless chores, one arm still cradling the infant at her breast. Unrelenting, headstrong or mad, her husband continues to strike wood against metal. Jeremiah sees no change in its configuration. Invincible, it taunts the would-be smith. But guided by some exquisite obsession, he persists.

Overhead, vultures glide in wide sweeping circles, surveying life, espying death, smelling it down below in the bottomless, sulfurous pits where the corpses of murdered street children are dumped. Many of the birds are now perched on roofs and tree limbs. Emboldened by some irresistible effluvia, a few make landfall. Waddling from side to side, wary and cunning, they will fight for the vilest scrap of carrion in their path. The leathery flutter of their wings sends chills down my spine.

Jeremiah returned to the gloomy depths of Gehenna looking for answers. He'd been perusing Spinoza's seminal work, *Ethics* and Einstein's Theory of Special Relativity. Separated by three centuries, the philosopher and the physicist had both studied relativity, the first to explore the metaphysical realm, the second to postulate immutable cosmic laws. They reached broadly similar conclusions, among them that perception depends on vantage point.

Spinoza buoyed his argument by demystifying the universe

and proposing -- swiftly earning him excommunication and centuries of Jewish and Christian hostility -- that much of human consciousness is based, not on fact, but on how we are conditioned to interpret the occurrence of *being*. There are no wrong answers, he proposes, only divergent opinions which are themselves blurred by conformity to *encoded* beliefs, not congenital concepts. He may have been the first to suggest that truth is in the mind's eye of the beholder.

Einstein also theorized that reality is merely an illusion, *"albeit a very persistent one."* He went a step further. He declared that perceptions can actually alter reality and the experience of *being*. Jeremiah had an opportunity to test this strange concept, not in the perfect geometry of space, nor in the sterile labyrinths of Cartesian logic, but in a realm that has grown and spilled over its own boundaries like a gangrenous sore, far from the synthetic harmony of a world where the well-to-do live in stifling isolation.

It was still dark as Jeremiah worked his way to the bridge. He came upon sleepy-eyed children pulling heavy loads, sweaty gaunt men packed like sardines in rickety trucks belching black smoke, half submerged under the garbage they were ferrying from one end of the chasm to the other.

Huddled like newborn pups against the scurfy wall of an abandoned building, young boys slept, their arms crossed against the chill of night, their fingers clasping their shoulders. Others, stirring from a thin, turbulent slumber, were getting ready, in lieu of breakfast, to take the long and excruciating way out of reality by surrendering to glue. Further on, resting on a bed of filthy rags near the gutter, a woman dozed fitfully with an infant at her breast while an older child begged for scraps of food and wiped an ever-runny nose on the sleeve of a threadbare jersey.

Ahead, past the bridge, in a huge crater-like depression teeming with vultures, Jeremiah found toddlers and young teens feeding on garbage. Knee-deep in steaming mountains of waste and competing with the loathsome winged scavengers, another group of youngsters rummaged for a meal, a slipper, perhaps a broken toy to brighten an otherwise joyless childhood.

And when he ventured past the festering hollow, Jeremiah chanced upon a living ghost. He had no other words to describe her. She has no name. Madness robs people of all identity. Madness, in her case, further sharpens the alienation, the anonymity. She has no name. She has earned the scorn of her own wretched kind and she will pass in this dimension and from this moment in time unnoticed, even by her fellow specters. Surely, a name, a common moniker would give her substance, if not legitimacy. But she's been forgotten. Insanity and amnesia have mercifully yanked her from the clutches of reality. Yet she is real, irritatingly tangible, the symbol and victim of the dysfunctional society that spawned her. Shunned, loathed, she inspires revulsion, not pity, for she is unrepentant, defiant in her grotesque cardboard palace, amid the debris, the scraps of metal, the offal on which she feeds, the useless memories that haunt her still, come rain or come shine, come hell or high water.

Her partner-in-grime, ageless, toothless, feral and mad, too mad to erect her own shelter, sits by her companion's side or steals forty winks on the naked pavement, her hands pressed together to form a cushion under her cheek. Wielding a yard of rubber tubing, or an old broom, she chases after man and specter with equal fury, a menacing fist raised against oncoming traffic and snickering children, striking the ground with anger and bewilderment, no, with exasperation, spitting at passersby, pelting them with invectives. Sometimes folly crests like an open flame fanned by wind and a torrent of tears drenches her grand-motherly face. Overwhelmed by the sheer intensity of her exasperation, she calms down and tunes in briefly on the world around her; then she resumes her silent vigil, a lifeless gaze now focused on an all-consuming void.

One day, four policemen swooped down on Gehenna and smashed the paper, string and plastic scaffolding her friend had erected. Even a place of torment such as Gehenna, Jeremiah mused, has its heartless enforcers, its dim-witted disciplinarians. The woman put up a fierce battle but the enforcers prevailed. Trampled by uncaring feet, the decimated remains of her flimsy abode were carted away and thrust aside under the bridge where trash and raw sewage eventually end up. In the end, the authorities showed some mercy: She was allowed to bed down on the bare ground and fend for herself.

Up the road, in the narrow, slop-splattered alley that hugs the flanks of an old church, a man writhed in drug-induced agony. Frothing at the mouth, his eyes on fire, he crumbled to the ground and let out a blood-curdling wail. Clawing at the demons that tormented him, thrashing about, he rolled into the gutter and narrowly missed being hit by a speeding garbage truck.

Safe in their pews, the faithful were being treated to the grand spectacle of a pre-dawn mass. "*Dominus vobiscum*," said the priest. "*Et cum spiritu tuo*," the faithful responded, mercifully unmindful, if only for a brief moment in their beleaguered lives, of the pervading godlessness that surrounds them.

Around the corner, propped against a fence, a group of cripples flaunted their grotesque infirmities. Unruffled, bystanders the faithful, the penitent, the aimless and the lost, the discarded and the redundant, stepped over them like so much rubbish. Across the street, sprawled on the ground, a young woman breast-fed her newborn as three older daughters, sired by three different men, plied the beggar's trade.

Are these scenes of utter madness, Jeremiah reflected, or was he observing prosaic reality through the prism of his own budding psychosis?

As he pondered the question, Jeremiah nearly tripped on the cadavers of three children. They lay prone, splotches of dried blood streaking their faces. They'd been hogtied and gagged and shot, gangland-style in the back of the head.

The only thing that separates "God" and his creation is a dissimilar perspective. Relativity prevents either from switching places. In Gehenna, as in the parallel universe Jeremiah inhabits, where heaven and hell coexist in perilous proximity, right and wrong are less sharply defined. For the powerful, the privileged, the favored, the free, the well-fed who squander their freedom by abdicating to the tyranny of convention, truth remains the stronger of two or more conflicting views. For the poor, the disenfranchised, the forgotten, the unloved, the nameless and the ghouls and the zombies that haunt our conscience, the truth is a useless paradox, like relativity. Don't look for answers, Jeremiah kept telling himself. Don't look for reason. All you'll find is nature, cruel and unmoved, further debased by the aggregate interests and avarice of the dominant elite.

It was now nearly dawn but the sun had yet to rise behind Gehenna's battered ramparts. An ashen darkness still clung like a shroud over its higher elevations. Up since the cocks' first crow, Zion (Jeremiah gave her that name to commemorate the fleeting apparition) raced down the sheer, narrow footpath leading to the murky waters of the creek below. Pressed to her bosom, swaddled in an old piece of cloth and still asleep, her infant daughter seemed oblivious to it all. The footpath is overrun with hazards but Zion knows every crag, every loose pebble, every muddy ledge along the way. She's made the perilous trek a thousand times or more since the birth of her baby, six months ago, and she negotiates each obstacle with the agility of a veteran climber.

Laden with her precious cargo, a pail of water now balanced atop her head, Zion turned around and clambered back uphill. Midway, she stopped to catch her breath. She must manage her strength. She's pregnant with her second child and she's hardly eaten in the past two days. But Zion is no stranger to privation. Pain no longer daunts her. She has her baby to care for. Another little one is on the way in five months or less, she's not sure.

Slowly, night's inky mantle dissolved, baring a pale orange sky. A new day had dawned, bringing a fresh surge of anticipation and energy. Emboldened, Zion resumed her arduous climb.

Zion is fourteen.

Reaching the summit, winded by the grueling ascent, Zion wiped her brow and surveyed her surroundings. Barely visible in morning's timid glow, familiar and inescapable, an unobstructed scene of utter barrenness stretched before her, a landscape of squalor and malignancy and evil that the thick haze failed to conceal. Above it, out-of-focus, floating like a mirage over the distant haze, stretched the gleaming spires and gables of an inaccessible, forbidden upperworld. Behind her, balancing precariously on the edge of a narrow bluff overgrown with stinkweed, sat the ramshackle hut Zion calls home. Straddling a scaffolding of rotting wood pylons and corroded iron beams under which a small emaciated dog and a palsied cat cowered, the windowless shack stands defiant in its vulnerability, a symbol of the paradox that is Gehenna.

Zion blows out the quivering flame of an old kerosene lamp and fans away the acrid emanations. She lays the sleeping infant on the floor, gently propping her head against a cardboard box where she keeps all of her possessions. There's a rag doll, an old discolored dress, a small bundle of used baby clothes, an old photograph, a broken comb, a tin of cereal, a jar of brown sugar in which tiny yellow ants have taken up residence, a cross fashioned from popsicle sticks, a faded prayer book frontispiece in which an enraptured Aryan Christ is seen levitating above a sea of mesmerized disciples.

Zion strikes a match, ignites kindling in the hollow of a cinder block and stirs a thin gruel of rice and water into a pitted metal bowl. She stopped breast-feeding her daughter when she became pregnant with her second child. Underweight, her ashen skin pocked with mosquito bites, the baby girl suffers from malnutrition. Zion looks at her daughter with a mixture of tenderness and despair as her own childhood, barely tasted, irretrievably lost, comes back to haunt her.

Zion is the embodiment of innocence undone, childhood imperiled and corrupted by poverty, neglect and hopelessness. Soft-spoken and unassuming, she reluctantly relives the nightmare by evoking it at Jeremiah's urging. Despite the horror it inspires, her narration is childlike, flat. Her voice betrays neither anger nor sorrow. She smiles timidly instead, perhaps to hide the shame and pity she feels, not for herself, but for those who so sadistically withheld their love and deprived her of her dignity.

Jeremiah asks her what she desires most and he feels instantly shamed by the vacuity of his question. Fixing a gaze of unfathomable emptiness at some distant point in space, giving Jeremiah time to ponder his lack of tact, then turning tenderly to the toddler nestled in her arms and patting her own belly, the child-mother replies,

"I have nothing and I have everything. I can't ask for less or for more."

In Zion's world, nothing and everything are usually too much to bear.

Morning alit -- or something akin to morning. A faint gray glow crept out of an overcast horizon. The glow was not bright enough to disperse the misty tendrils of fog that hung like wispy ghosts over the desolation.

Gehenna, like fungus, has spread tentacle-like, sprouting squalid slums along muddy ridges and down the slopes of dank garbage-strewn ravines. It's in one such slum, nicknamed Limón by the locals because of the jade-green stream of sludge that runs through it that Jeremiah came across Angelica. He found her sitting at the edge of a cot, her feet pitted by insect bites and glistening skin lesions, in a shed under a leaking corrugated sheet metal roof held up by rotting wooden beams.

In a corner of the room, under the pallid rays of a 40-watt bulb around which a squadron of moths kept circling, propped on a table littered with rags and old newspapers, rested a tall, garishly painted plaster figurine, a Madonna and child whose introspective, tortured gaze, frozen skyward where God is said to dwell, exuded pain and disillusionment, betrayal and stupefaction. Every once in a while, almost mechanically, the girl cast a forlorn glance at the Virgin Mary, perhaps for reassurance. But in her large brown eyes all Jeremiah saw were false hopes and broken promises.

This time Jeremiah said nothing. Assailed by a jumble of emotions, he just looked at her cherub face. He wanted to hug her and, to absorb her within his being for warmth and reassurance. But he didn't dare. Instead, he took her little hand in his and held it for a while. Angelica blushed, looked at the bare concrete floor and sighed.

"Take her away from this place," her mother pleaded.

"Take her? Away? Where? How? What do I know about the transmigration of souls," Jeremiah lamented, waving the mother away. "When was the last time I rescued someone from a nightmare?" Then he thought: what if this is a trap? What if Angelica is a succubus, an evil spirit, a demon who morphs into cherubim and seraphs? Jeremiah understood what sophistry can do to distort judgment, to cripple reason, to inspire fear, to justify cynicism. And as he looked at Angelica's innocent face, he chose discretion over valor. He ran out and burst into tears.

Outside, the vultures, the ever-present vultures, resumed their abominable vigil, gliding overhead like black-winged demons at a Witches' Sabbath, awaiting death, smelling it, tasting it. Surely, Jeremiah reflected, even God must find Limón a very bitter fruit.

THE FOOT FETISH

I believe in compulsory cannibalism.
If people were forced to eat what they killed,
there would be no more wars.
Abbie Hoffman

"Tired, aching feet slowing you down? Burning, itchy toes making you frown? Are you plagued with calluses and bunions, cracks as wide as canyons? Or are you simply out of pace? Don't be your own arch-enemy. Drag your heels no more. Put some bounce in your stride, pep in your gait. Let us anoint your feet. We'll give them Hermes's wings. Our dedicated, licensed practitioners will lavish you with the treatment of your life. So take that precious first step and run -- don't just walk. We're conveniently located a skip and a hop from anywhere. For an early appointment call The Foot Fetish at 1-800-TOE-LINE. A unique twist in foot care."

In a rare moment of self-pity, Ethan Caruthers turns to the pain in his feet. He winces. They have ached forever, it seems. Sly

59

and unpredictable on busy days when mind conquers matter, the pain returns, tenacious and all-consuming after dark. But whining is not part of the Caruthers temperament. The Caruthers are a stoic, iron-willed lot not given to martyrdom, an ancient family with an emblazoned colonial past, now ruled by Major Archibald Spencer Caruthers, his father -- whom Ethan still calls "sir" -- and his mother, Lady Sarah Covington Caruthers, a woman of exceptional beauty in her youth, now fending off the ravages of time and tropics with heavy makeup and triple gins and tonic. Ethan Alcott Caruthers, their only son (more by accident than choice) quickly learns to manage the chilliness of the Caruthers code, "like a man," a lesson further beaten into him with his parents' consent by Jesuit bullies at Holy Cross Lyceum. But years of neglect, ill-fitting shoes -- his mother had insisted that small feet are a mark of good breeding -- and half a dozen toes broken chasing after crabs on some distant reef had claimed a cruel toll.

Caruthers studies the leaflet and smiles. He seeks out the young hawker who providentially thrust it in his hand as he strolled on his lunch hour, but the hawker is gone, swallowed by a sea of noontime amblers.

Ethan dials the number on his cell phone.

"The Foot Fetish. May I help you?" The timbre is both suggestive and businesslike. Perhaps it's the way she enunciates "fetish," accentuating ever so vaguely on a lusty "t" with all the prim affectation of a Soho fellatrix. Alas, Caruthers doesn't notice such things. His upbringing denies him the privilege of an impious mind, much less the fun of being lured by innuendo, real or imagined. Now 24, Caruthers inexplicably had sex only three times, first with the maid in the broom closet, when he was just thirteen. A year later, his first cousin Rachel Elizabeth seduced him behind a patch of wisteria and daffodils at the

Droitwich estate where the clan seeks yearly refuge from the rigors of the Malay summer. His last escapade took place in the arms of a doe-eyed Sinhalese teen prostitute whose expert services wound up costing Ethan Alcott Caruthers several million units of penicillin to his pink English bum.

"My feet are killing me," Caruthers says, mixing wit and metaphor.

"I have a cancellation at four-thirty on Tuesday. Will that do?" Fluid, mellifluous, the voice paints lips of glossy crimson, full, pouting, a heart-shaped opening behind which lurks a pearly smile and a playful tongue, all of which Caruthers ignores in favor of his metatarsals.

"Yes. I'll be there."

"Your name?"

Caruthers complies as soothing thoughts of pain relieved dance in his head.

A faded beauty still lingers in old Chinatown, deep in the shadow of Singapore's cut-glass, steel and neon-lit skyline, far from the lush gardens, vivid orchid-clad esplanades and immaculate tree-lined boulevards. Here, narrow streets and cul-de-sacs are home to medicine halls and shop houses and pleasure dens where no perversion is denied, where no vice is too odious to contemplate. Caruthers often ambles past their red and gold vaulted porticos, unable to muster the courage to go in, preferring to be vicariously thrilled by both the lure of temptation and the empty redemption of self-denial. He lingers there when the doors are ajar, taking in the tang of freshly ground spices, the heady aroma of rose water and jasmine, and the faint but unmistakable scent of lusting bodies wafting past him from the cool shadows beyond. He will never cross the threshold. Instead, he collects the images and sensations and stores them for later retrieval and solitary use in the privacy of his bathroom. While his libido has escaped unscathed, the fear of risking yet another loathsome chancre has forever dulled any penchant for promiscuity.

Caruthers turns left on Sago Street. Songbirds in bamboo cages, paper lanterns and slender poles heavy with drying clothes sway from upper-level windows. Calligraphers and scribes sit huddled on the pavement, gilding strips of lucky red paper with gold ideograms, or taking dictation from the old and the unschooled. On Smith Street, wooden sculptures of deities as ancient as the dynasties of carvers that gave them life stand the test of time and faith amid papier-mâché replicas of earthly effigies destined to go up in flames at the funeral of some venerable patriarch.

Outside, the Sri Mariamman Temple, where cherry and lime-green painted gods, goddesses and sacred beasts guard the towering gateway, a soothsayer burns aromatic incense and consults the oracles. The swish of saris, the jingle of glass bead bracelets and the stirring strains of Tamil love songs fill the air.

Caruthers stops and beckons a trained parrot to pick out a fortune card from a brass bowl.

"Never raise arms when washing hands lest water trickle down sleeves," the card warns with cryptic sarcasm. Baffled, Caruthers urges the parrot to do better. The bird squawks with impatience, sifts grudgingly through the bowl with his beak, picks another card and hands it to Caruthers.

"Only a hair's breadth separates paradise from hell."

"That's more like it," Caruthers smiles, his spirituality appeased.

She is very young, a raven-haired beauty in a jade-green silk dress with side slits that bare alabaster thighs. Her eyes twinkle playfully as she glides toward him.

"May I help you?"

"My name is Caruthers. I have an appointment."

"Welcome to the Foot Fetish, Mr. Caruthers. I am Koo Mai. Do sit down, won't you? Someone will be with you shortly."

Koo Mai has more, much more than a lascivious *"t"* to her credit.

The phone trills softly. Koo Mai picks up the receiver and answers the call in a singsong of Malay and Chinese. She turns to Caruthers.

"Dr. Vollbrecht will see you now. Second floor, first door on you right."

Vollbrecht is in his fifties, a Curt Jurgens clone, handsome and suave. He wears an immaculate white frock. Self-assured and focused, he handles the scalpel with skill. With each deft stroke, a small mound of dead skin shavings rises in a white ceramic bowl before him.

"Have you ever heard the expression, 'dead weight,'" Vollbrecht asks with noticeable pride. He lifts the bowl and pours out the contents on a scale. "Four ounces!" Vollbrecht is beaming. "Do you realize you've just shed a quarter of a pound -- and it all came from your feet?"

Caruthers wiggles his toes and caresses the baby-smooth contours of his soles, heels and big toes. He feels positively rejuvenated.

Vollbrecht smiles. "Miss Tung will tend to you now. Su Lin," he calls out.

Su Lin, a shapely adolescent as delicate as a bisque figurine, kneels before Caruthers, raises one of his legs and proceeds to lick and suck his toes. Caruthers stiffens, a mixture of surprise and embarrassment etched upon his face, a blissful jolt shooting up his rectum and radiating to his scrotum. He looks quizzically at Vollbrecht, averting his eyes from the spectacle of this voluptuous if bizarre seduction.

"That's all right, think nothing of it. It's included in the fee. Besides, it's standard practice in modern chiropody. And that's just for starters."

Reassured, if not altogether convinced, Caruthers relaxes and Su Lin resumes her carnal commerce. Feigning indifference, he picks up a dog-eared edition of The Economist.

Koo Mai joins Su Lin, kneels beside her, unzips Caruthers' pants and loosens his belt. Her intentions are less than honorable, Caruthers surmises, but he is ready for her -- prudence be damned, to hell with everything. He closes his eyes, his chin drops and his lips part to receive Su Lin's strawberry tongue and the fullness of her mouth upon his. Su Lin's nimble caresses help Caruthers rise to the occasion and Koo Mai takes him in her mouth. Her head bobs up and down like a penitent before the Wailing Wall. Rapture is near. He lets it come. Pleasure slowly swells within him, submerging him. Bliss. Oblivion. Then pain.

The pain is real, obstinate, all-pervading.

Koo Mai is dining on a tumescent, mauve, glistening shaft, the very one she had so greedily milked, now an alien, mangled, lifeless bloody shank that had once been his.

He cries out, a feeble whimper, a would-be scream stifled by horror and disbelief, the kind of mournful, guttural lament that dies in one's throat when nightmares take over.

Pain turns to agony.

Su Lin has ripped his big toe clear off the bone and is now tearing into his Achilles tendon with her bare teeth. Blood trickles from the corners of her mouth -- his blood -- and he can hear the crunching sounds of sinew and cartilage being chewed to a gritty pulp.

"Noooo," he shrieks, his face contorted, eyes ablaze, arms flailing against the steely grip of his tormentors. "I beg you."

Vollbrecht, a *bon vivant* to his manicured fingertips, goes for a more substantial cut of meat and digs into Caruthers' mid-section.

Su Lin now attacks his calf, rupturing muscle, severing veins and arteries, shearing nerves, swallowing whole chunks of featureless flesh with shark-like frenzy.

Caruthers closes his eyes, thinking himself in Hades. Or in the grips of a nightmare, as it were. He is being devoured alive.

Ethan Alcott Caruthers's remains are found on Gull Crescent Lane the next morning, the toeless stumps that had once been his feet oozing blood, his penis ripped clear off, his belly a gaping, eviscerated, festering cavity in which maggots and rats are now feasting.

I wake up tasting blood, my tongue savagely bitten in the course of a phantasm that has run amok, an exquisite hallucination bound to take me closer yet to the brink.

ONE NIGHT IN COPÁN

The Lords of Xibalba burst out laughing;
they were dying of laughter; they writhed from pain
in their stomach, in their blood, and in their bones,
caused by their laughter, all the Lords of Xibalba laughed.
The Popol Vuh

An eerie pall of mystery wafts over Copán late at night when villagers slumber and the ghosts of the mighty Maya awaken in otherworldly darkness. Their presence, wraithlike, elusive like the last frames of a dissolving dream, had often kept me awake, or stirred me from a paralyzing sleep. But nothing could have prepared me for what I'd experience on a moonless night in February 2006. It is so farfetched an event, so devastating a blow to my self-view as a skeptic, a debunker, that I waited almost a year before I told anyone -- and only on condition of anonymity.

I'd paid the bill, left Doña Delsey her usual tip and was about to leave the El Sesteo cantina where I'd dined that evening when the lights went out. This is not an uncommon occurrence in Honduras but one that, depending on duration, elicits emotions ranging from exasperation to contempt. I'd left my flashlight in my studio at the other end of town in a sparsely populated residential area overlooking the lush Copán River Valley. And I knew better than to venture in the dark, risking life and limb in an attempt to negotiate my way back to my flat across cobbled alleys and rain-filled potholes.

Instead, feeling full and in need of a workout, I headed in the opposite direction and proceeded down the main road that leads out of the village and runs alongside the Archeological Park, less than a kilometer away.

It was pitch-black but the star-studded sky above sparkled like a diamond-studded wreath. Suddenly, as I neared the Park's main gate, a bright object appeared out of nowhere. Far brighter than the stars, encircled by a bluish metallic halo, it began zigzagging erratically at unimaginable speeds. Then it stopped, sloped to a lower altitude, and hovered motionless for about ninety seconds. I calculated its position to be directly above the Temple of the Hieroglyphic Stairway, a sixty-five foot high terraced pyramid made of stones carved with Mayan pictograms, many yet to be decoded. It was then that I noticed that the object was elliptical in shape and ringed with pulsating, oscillating lights. I believe I saw a humanoid figure peering from one of the portholes that lined the perimeter of the craft. Then, like a flash, the object zoomed away, shrank to a shimmering point of light and vanished in the immense starry blackness of space.

I never mentioned the incident to anyone, fearing that I might come across as a lunatic or a drunkard. I recorded the incident in far greater detail in a small notebook which I then placed in a sealed envelope marked "OPEN ONLY UPON MY DEATH." I posted the envelope and its contents to my attorney in Paris.

On December 30, 2007, I e-mailed my old Honduran friend and colleague, Pablo Beltrán. I summarized the events I'd witnessed nearly a year earlier and gave Beltrán permission, should he deem it of interest, to relate my story on condition that my name be changed or withheld.

Beltrán did just that in a column dated January 1, 2008 and published in El Mundo, the leading daily where he works.

"What have I done!" he lamented the next day. "I've been swamped with calls -- fifteen or more -- all asking for your address, all demanding to know when and where the sighting took place. The UFO Club of San Pedro is organizing an outing to Copán on Saturday ... they plan to spend the night outdoors. Hondurans love the occult, UFOs, prophecies, witchcraft, voodoo and all that nonsense. Should I give this story continuity or drop it? One caller said that the notebook to be read after your death must surely contain details of your encounter with an 'extraterrestrial.' The column is a hit but what do I do next? Can you tell me more?"

"Pablito" I responded, "stay with the story but keep my name and whereabouts out of it. You and my attorney are the only people who know anything about this 'encounter.' I'm weighing your request for additional details and might provide you with some in the coming days. My eagerness to tell all is dampened by circumspection. It'll be interesting to see if the other dailies pick up on your column and whether Roberto Hidalgo [La Republica's Copán correspondent] mentions it in one of his self-serving commentaries. Meanwhile, hoteliers will do brisk business as the UFO Club converges on Copán for a night or two of sky-gazing...."

"I'm in Marseille. I had a fabulous bouillabaisse and feasted on escargots in garlic butter. With some time to kill, I visited the Chateau d'If, the tiny rocky island fortress where Edmond

Dantès, the semi-fictional hero of the *Count of Monte Cristo* was imprisoned and from which, the Dumas novel purports, he managed to escape. French revolutionary statesman and erotic novelist, Honoré de Mirabeau, and half a dozen other notable inmates, were not quite as lucky. Some languished in the catacomb-like prison for years, among them Protestants, anti-royalists; an aristocrat who maintained a lifelong homosexual liaison with *Monsieur,* the brother of Louis XIV (and seduced one the king's bastard sons); and a man falsely accused of bringing the plague to Marseille. Ah, if only some of your colonels and generals could have met a similar fate ....

"In the meantime, you might consider penning a second column based on the responses and reactions your first one elicited among readers. That's one way of giving the story an extra pair of wings."

In an e-mail dated January 4, Beltrán wrote: "I've been re-reading all the UFO background material you sent me, while fending off a new wave of frantic calls from readers. THEY BELIEVE! They seem to have a *need* to believe! Yesterday was a strange and freaky day. First, there was a nationwide power failure that lasted well over thirty minutes. Then it began to rain heavily. The torrential downpour was accompanied by howling winds that uprooted trees and leveled countless shanties. Well, you can imagine, the phone kept ringing, with readers asking *me* if the daylong deluge had *'anything to do with what your friend saw at the Archeological Park.'* It took quite a bit of doing to convince people that the freaky tempest was in no way connected to your sightings. People here are scared shitless. Some blame you for *'interfering with the supernatural.'* This is a riot! Members of the San Pedro UFO Club are converging on Copán. They will be spending two nights at the Park's main gate, binoculars, telescopes, picnic baskets and all. I think my last column was the most widely read of my entire career. I don't know whether to embrace you or curse you"

"Pablito," I answered, "How amusing that the power failure is being blamed on other than deterministic earthly events. Few UFO sightings have ever coincided with massive blackouts. I don't have to remind you, most electric service interruptions in Honduras are either weather-related, the result of human error or deliberate tampering by the power company to compensate for overload conditions. Anyway, I'm stunned by the volume and stridency of the responses your column inspired.

"After careful reflection, I've decided to prepare a 'second round' that is certain to deliver a knockout punch and make UFO believers -- and skeptics alike -- see stars. I'll send it in after a decent interval. Let's let the fever rise then subside for a while."

On January 10, I e-mailed Beltrán:

"Pablito, I've been thinking. Adding, however cautiously, to my earlier disclosures puts me in the awkward position of saying far more than I should. I'm still alive and a working journalist. I worry not only about my reputation, which would be compromised should my identity accidentally be leaked, but also about a man in Copán whose astounding revelations left me bewildered and apprehensive. I'll try. But that's as far as I'll go for the time being.

"You can appreciate how difficult it was for a hard-boiled cynic like me to accept what I'd witnessed last February. I felt compelled to supplement what might have been a mirage, an optical illusion -- or a brief descent into madness -- with some verifiable evidence. I needed to know the truth not only to validate my own sanity but to add some measure of solid reality to an occurrence dismissed by skeptics as 'natural phenomena' or 'psychosis' and by believers as foreshadowing apocalypse.

"The next day, I gained admittance to the Archeological Park about an hour before closing time. Dressed in dark clothes, I meandered through the Park's vast expanse like a tourist, shooting pictures, taking notes and attracting no undue attention. At about 5 p.m., I hid in a dark and narrow cavity linking two crumbling stone structures in a remote area behind the Ball Court. I waited for night to engulf the Park before venturing out into the open.

"By 9 p.m., nothing had happened and I began to feel like a fool. Worse, the cold chill of the ancient stone walls against which I'd huddled for more than an hour permeated my being. I knew a way out of the Park by climbing over the collapsed remains of an ancient parapet at the eastern edge of the ruins and scaling down a steep incline covered with dense underbrush. It was dark and I realized that this route would place me some two kilometers from the main road and in densely forested terrain.

"I was mulling over my next move when I felt a sudden pressure in my ears. The pressure billowed into a very low-pitched hum that throbbed through my chest. The hum intensified and it was then that I observed the same 'object' I'd seen the night before hovering about 30 meters over the Hieroglyphic Stairway. A bright, thin, pulsating laser-like green shaft of light shot out from under the craft, bathing the top rungs of the Stairway with an eerie glow. This incredible spectacle lasted about three minutes. My heart was pounding and I pinched myself to make sure I wasn't in the throes of a horrible nightmare. No sooner did I realize that what I'd seen was real, terrifyingly real, than the beam of light receded slowly and telescoped back into the belly of the craft. The craft then shot upward at a speed beyond human comprehension -- and which would have pulverized any human occupant -- and vanished.

"I was now bathing in sweat, breathless, dizzy. I must have passed out for the next thing I remember was being revived by Eusebio.

"'What are you doing here,' I asked.

"'No! What are *you* doing here?' he replied, grabbing me by the wrists, with more than a hint of annoyance in his voice.

"I told Eusebio what I'd witnessed the night before and what had compelled me to return to the site the night after. I asked him if what I'd seen was real and, if so, whether he could explain it.

"Eusebio, whose impoverished hamlet nestling near the Guatemalan border I'd visited several times, knew I could be trusted. But he hesitated. He then pressed his lips against my ear and murmured something about 'ancient prophecies,' 'tribal payback,' and the 'imminent return of the Lords of Xibalba to reclaim the land from the usurpers.'

"I urged him to elaborate. He smiled gently but said nothing. I left Copán the next day on the 6 a.m. bus to San Pedro Sula and flew out of Honduras.

"Pablito, I've told you infinitely more than I should have. The rest, which I resolved never to reveal while I'm alive, is detailed in a letter written in Mayan symbols. The letter now rests in my attorney's safe.

P.S. *Has there been any reaction to your columns from the military?*"

A day later I received an animated e-mail from Beltrán.

"… Another stampede of stargazers is charging toward Copán tomorrow. They must first obtain special permission to spend the night at the Park. They will be charged an extra fee and won't be allowed to take in any food or beverages. It's a riot: A reader called claiming that the U.S. Army is using the humming sound you described in Afghanistan. The humming, he said, becomes so intense that "insurgents" burst out of their caves screaming in agony. He also asserted that the U.S. 'reverse-engineered the humming effect' from the UFO that crashed in Roswell, New Mexico in 1947....

P.S. *German Monteblanco, of La Nacíon, published a cautious editorial based on my original article. He takes the UFO theory seriously. Strangely, the Honduran military have been mum on the subject. The military here don't read. They just listen to the radio or watch TV or get drunk or torture people.... It's the readers who are out of control. They hunger for more. What else do I tell them? Who is 'Eusebio'?"*

"Pablito," I answered on January 17, "you've asked me, justifiably, to endow 'Eusebio' with more than just skin, bone and marrow. I hesitated this long for reasons that will become apparent. But since your readers are clamoring like a pack of wolves for more of the flesh of this extraordinary story, and to prevent anyone christened Eusebio anywhere in the greater Copán River Valley from being hassled, possibly victimized, I can tell you this much: 'Eusebio' is an alias. He told me that himself. His real name is unpronounceable. Several weeks after I decamped from Copán, I learned from a tribal counselor in Corralitos that 'Eusebio' had disappeared under mysterious circumstances and has never been seen again. One can only wonder whether he was assassinated, a fate shared by so many of his kinfolks, or whether he left Honduras for a better life elsewhere.

"In retrospect, 'Eusebio,' whom I'd befriended on previous visits to Copán, seemed more aloof, remote, more distant than his fellow Maya. He was short and wiry, and his coal-black eyes would often turn milky when the sun hit them a certain way. I never paid much attention to this peculiarity, which I dismissed as an optical illusion or ophthalmological oddity. 'Eusebio' spoke softly, almost in a whisper, and his words, often ambig-

74

uous or allegorical, conveyed ideas that were sometimes so perplexing and impenetrable that I dismissed them as the ramblings of a mystic high on magic mushrooms.

"I also remarked that few of his cohorts called him 'Eusebio.' They preferred to address him as *U-wach-euse*, a name I inferred was a reverential title in Kakchiquel, Q'uiche or one of the twenty-odd Mayan languages spoken in the region. I looked up the name in an encyclopedia of linguistics; my search proved fruitless.

"I remember Eusebio with great fondness. He was a gentle, self-effaced character who spoke in riddles when asked probing questions, and who had the uncanny faculty of vanishing and reappearing as if he had wings or could travel through walls. I will never know why he was at the Archeological Park that fateful night and what special meaning his words conveyed."

"The recent UFO citing in Stephenville, Texas," I wrote Pablo Beltrán on January 21, "hit the big news, with CNN and other networks milking the story dry. People are crawling out of the woodwork, eager to tell their own tales. Stanton Friedman, a respected astrophysicist I first met when I was managing editor of Aerospace America magazine in New York, insists that the U.S. government's studied indifference is contrived to trivialize phenomena that have captivated and troubled people for decades. If UFOs are not prototypes of secret U.S. military research into, say, anti-gravity technology, Friedman argues, they must be extraterrestrial. Predictably, the government is not commenting.

"My own take on this affair is that if these unidentified objects are not human in origin, their existence poses a grave threat to monotheistic religions.

"Anyway, mounting worldwide interest in UFOs could justify another column in which you solicit reader feedback.

What you collect should offer revealing insights into the psyche, fears and fantasies of a cross-section of your public -- all of which you could then synthesize into yet another column."

Pablo Beltrán let the story die. He never told me why and I never asked. Perhaps he got tired of the phone calls, the frenzy his columns had created. Nor would I ever tell him, or anyone else what I'd itched to reveal from the start: that Eusebio came from the planet Euse in a distant outpost of the spiral galaxy closest to the Milky Way, Messier 31, some 2.5 million light-years from Earth in the Andromeda constellation; that he'd added the suffix "bio" to his name to denote *life*, and that his Euseian ancestors had shared their secrets of astronomy, mathematics and calendric sciences with the ancient Maya.

It is not for me to echo Eusebio's expressions of sorrow and anger at the poverty, alienation and dismal prospects of the Maya, or of his people's age-old yearning to punish those who continue to mistreat their descendants. Nor can I ever admit to having seen Eusebio on the night of our last encounter emerge from an aperture in the hewn rock wall behind which I'd been hiding (or was it a window into another dimension?) and into which he coalesced and turned to stone, his fingers still clutching my wrists. Don't take my word for it. If you ever visit the Park and look carefully, you can find him, frozen in time, his brow furrowed, his eyes, half-closed, staring at infinity.

Only time will tell whether the ancient Maya's predictions of a new Xibalba within the next decade or so are accurate, or the delirious hallucinations of madmen.

Before me, relived in cryptic iconography and faded hieroglyphics, was the colossal spectacle of genius exhausted, splendor humbled, enlightenment dimmed by a headlong rush toward cultural extinction. Conflict, ferocious blood-letting rituals, an obsession with death, overpopulation, deforestation, hunger, disease -- all had conspired to bring to a close an epoch of fabulous artistic expression and agonizing self-inquiry. The meteoric magnificence of the Maya is chronicled in the lichen-covered tabernacles, in the austerity of age-worn temples and ball-courts, in the enigmatic stares of petrified kings and demigods. The calamity that befell the city-state of Copán is witnessed in the bleak anonymity of unfinished monuments and abandoned stonework that lay scattered on the forest floor. Spectral vestiges of a powerful dynasty that began in the fifth century C. E. and ended in flight and dispersal four hundred years later, they may also be seen as a metaphor to the passion and the agony of a dispirited and rudderless posterity -- the modern-day Maya.

And as I gazed at the pyramids and temples and awe-inspiring statuary, I asked myself what sort of future awaits these time travelers. Past is prelude. Xibalba is not a mystical destination. It's a "circumstance," as Eusebio had called it, "an unavoidable and unending status quo."

LET ME TELL YOU ABOUT MAX

I'm mad between long intervals of horrible sanity.
I feel no pain when madness crests.
Keith Sidney "Max" Pontifex

There's an island where fish have wings and birds dive in the blue for their favorite catch, where men, groping for self-realization, blinded by the sun but scarcely enlightened by their colonial past, prey on each-other the better to cope with a common nightmare.

It was serendipity, not purpose or plan that first brought me to Stonewall. I would call this small island home for a decade or so as I searched for Shangri-La and surrendered lustfully to its siren call. Beyond its golden shores and the languid cadence of its ways, the world turned, and each rotation witnessed the dawning of human hopes and the demise of reason. Man was neither smarter nor more depraved than he'd ever been -- just more inventive, brazen. It was a ten-year period defined by momentous events long since forgotten or demoted to the back pages of history: The Watergate scandal. The raid on Entebbe.

The Chernobyl nuclear disaster. The disintegration of the Space Shuttle Challenger seventy-three seconds after takeoff. In Edmond, Oklahoma, Patrick Sherrill had gone "postal," killed fourteen co-workers and committed suicide. The Iran-Contra affair exposed yet another aspect of America's two-faced foreign policy.

In far-flung Stonewall, hidden from view under an azure canopy, as lush rain forests and mangroves spread their green tendrils all the way to the sea, things take place that escape scrutiny.

Fickle and self-absorbed, people entomb what they need not remember; they enshrine what they will not forget. Trifles take on mythical dimensions. Minor scandals feed the rumor mill; large ones invite outlandish, crowd-pleasing twaddle or ignite choleric tirades. Reminiscences apt to give people nightmares are promptly swept under a rug of selective amnesia. If you probe too deeply, if you resort to insightful conjecture, you will be greeted with suspicion or scorn. When doors slam shut, when friendly smiles turn to scowl, the truth, mind-boggling or hideous, lurks underfoot like a scorpion squeezing beneath a rock. Shadow politics and spin-doctoring are Stonewall's national sports. Boozing and cricket come a very distant third and fourth.

To the more astute observer, and for all its undeniable allure, Stonewall is eerily reminiscent of a theatrical backdrop; an all-too-perfect Hollywoodish "trompe l'oeil" that lures wanderers to its surreal perfection the way hibiscus and frangipani attract butterflies and bees. At first glance its exquisite beauty, the kind rhapsodized in syrupy sonnets and corny travelogues, can be hypnotic. Ringed by coastlines of striking majesty, silvery beaches here, rocky shores hammered by high surf there, it nestles, seductive and unruffled, a few square miles of old colonial charm seemingly unruffled, untouched by time. There's the ubiquitous clip-clop of horses' hooves on dusty back roads, whitewashed little churches, tumble down wooden rum shops where vacant-eyed loafers doze off in the noonday sun, and amiable peddlers who hawk worthless trinkets at jaded tourists. There's the redolence of grilled fish wafting from under the parasols of pushcart eateries; the cooling evening breezes, the graceful dawn-and-twilight flights of snowy egrets over lush, mist-covered uplands; the crisp, starlit nights and the leathery sound of batwings thrashing in the darkness.

Behind this idyllic setting unfold dramas unimagined by visitors, ignored or squelched by the press and warily entombed by the locals. Not far from the posh resorts, the crystal waters of the lagoons, the quaint restaurants and grungy guesthouses, pettifoggery, deceit, collusion and intimidation reign supreme while the locals live in sham unconcern.

Low tide. The surf tugs gently at the flotsam of sea moss, sun-bleached coral and broken shells scattered on the slick sandy shore. Purple clouds glide past a waxen moon, exposing an amber and cobalt sky. Pressing low against the sea, the remnants of a distant storm fade away as one last streak of lightning splashes the eastern horizon with a silvery glow.

Stillness fills my ears as I dream. Tree frogs suspend their call. Red-shelled crabs scuttle back to their burrows as the sun's smallest arc turns night into day. Shafts of light burst through the splintered shutters. A rooster crows in the distance. Doves respond, cooing their melancholy lilt. I make contact with reality when the voices down by the beach are not those that inhabit my dreams.

But I'm not here to dream. With every blink of the eye reality returns, clipped and spasmodic, like a badly edited film, like a parody of life in which nothing lies so well as the naked truth.

What I see and what my words convey somehow never seem to coincide. Syntax gets in the way. I'm now the prisoner of my own craft. Narrating a phantasm may be as risky as living it.

Rising from the ashtray, a thin, unwavering column of bluish smoke climbs from the smoldering mosquito-repelling coil to the ceiling where it shatters on impact. Inches away, a spider cruises by upside down, oblivious to the deadly wisps of insecticide that billow in its path. The fumes keep the mosquitoes at bay. I no longer get bitten. The local variety is fond of *whitey* only when his skin still bears the ghastly urban complexion of a newcomer. Eventually, they cease to visit and raid other abodes in search of fresh prey.

Cockroaches, bedbugs and spiders, the squatters of the insect world, are much less inventive. They move in for good.

Downstairs, the maids are setting tables. Sleepy-eyed and sullen, they meander in and out of the kitchen. I can hear the shuffle of dragging feet on the age-old tile floor. Dolores Wingate, the proprietor's wife, supervises the girls, issuing terse, monosyllabic orders from her room. She rarely leaves her room nowadays.

Mavis -- chambermaid, waitress, short-order cook and bartender -- mutters something in my direction. She stops halfway back to the kitchen. Looking elsewhere, wiping a lippy yawn, she asks, chopping her gs, "Yo be havin' coffee this mornin'?" I always have coffee; *every* mornin', but Mavis was instructed to ask. Just in case. The Wingates are such penny-pinchers.

Poached eggs stare back at me, lifeless, like the eyes of a dead fish. I fine-focus my field of view and I see myself in stereoscopic detail. My likeness beckons me to draw near. As I do, bleary-eyed, crumbling snippets of dream still fogging up my brain, my face looms larger in a yolk-yellow sea. I smile synthetically as if posing for a family portrait. It's a smile of my own creation. My lips are parted. That's all. It's a smile without cheer.

I poke the yolk and partake of breakfast. Repentance is where you find it. The eggs dissolve and submerge the shriveled, pinkie-sized sausages and undercooked home fries. Dolores' husband, Ephraim, turns on the radio. I don't like to be serenaded when I eat, least of all by Telemann or Handel. But Wingate has no passion for Debussy or Ravel.

Uninvited, a gecko leaps from the wall onto the faded plastic tablecloth. I overturn the sugar bowl. The little gray lizard with the big soulful eyes stops dead in its tracks, his senses aroused, his instincts on the alert. Hunger triumphs. A viscous tongue whips at the mound of sugar and retracts it laden with nourishing brown crystals.

Fuck Wingate.

Brooks is livid. The resident drunk, Whitney T. Brooks rooms here whenever he remembers the address or gets a lift from the local constabulary. Monthly checks keep him out of his family's hair in East Hampton, and he doesn't seem to give a shit, not about the hostility, the loneliness, the heat, the spiders, the monotony, the inescapable, unrelenting streams of Calypso music that swell and fade with the wind, the inky blackness of night.

"Filthy animal," Brooks snivels, recoiling with fear and revulsion. Coming from Brooks, it's a compliment. He won't look you in the eye. He cowers, instead, curling his upper lip like a dog begging to be kicked. He reeks of cheap rum. His teeth are yellow, his gaze reptilian, and a white slimy film coats the corners of his mouth. He shares my table. Day after day, breakfast, lunch and dinner. I don't have the heart to snub him.

Wingate lacks finesse. "Mixed-bloods," he calls them, sit under the wind chime at a large round table set in the center of the dining room. Those of "common stock," a special label reserved for people of dubious extraction, sit in clusters at tiny square tables, like satellites orbiting a mother ship. Miss Gwendolyn Peckham -- "Sussex, naturally" -- talkative and stone deaf, and more energetic than ten men half her eighty years, breaks bread with a young German drifter, Helmut Brunner, who speaks comic book English and never gets a chance to improve it in her presence.

Bates eats alone. His table faces a narrow wall from which hang reeking boughs of fan coral and a framed needlepoint inscription. *Victory Looms Brighter out of Darkness*, it proclaims with cryptic solemnity. Bates shuns the others. He eats with great haste, his nose in his plate, his eyes deep in thought. He always refolds the paper napkin on its original creases, gets up, mutters an apology and returns to his own dreams. He never sits in the sun.

Find me. I'm here, three, maybe four miles from town, past the old fishing village, off the winding road that girds the south coast. Turn left as you face north. Look for the sign.

THE BEARDED FIG TREE
BED & BREAKFAST
Ephraim Wingate, Proprietor

The old wooden placard swings at the end of a corroded yard of metal tubing extending from the eaves. It cries on windy nights. Stray cats often rally to its lugubrious wail.

The elements conspire; neglect finishes the job. The red corrugated iron roof sags. The verandah shows irreparable signs of fatigue. Devoured by wood worms, the balustrade threatens to collapse. Along the porch wall, hundreds of pockmarks erupt in tiny bloody splotches, each the silent witness of a swatted insect. Growing in untamed profusion, lime trees, breadfruit, hibiscus and bougainvillea soften the decadence.

Upstairs where I sleep, there are two single beds, lumpy and creaking, a narrow plywood closet that smells of old sweat and tree rot, a small desk and a wobbly chest of drawers lined with old newspapers perused a dozen times or more. Stand by as I quote from their pages from time to time.

Item:

"Owen Courtney, 47, of Marshall Hall, St. Lucy, pleaded guilty in the Fourth Assize Court to defecating on the steps of the Governor General's mansion. The infraction is reported to have occurred late on the night of 16 April. Justice Stewart L. Wifing, Q.C., deputy director for public prosecutions, appeared for the Crown.

"Mr. Frampton H. Cheltenham represented the defendant. Mr. Courtney could not explain why he had been drawn to that particular venue to respond to what he termed 'an urgent call of nature,' when an adjacent public lot, the very one from whence he had emerged, is dark and deserted at night. Sentencing has been postponed for a month and Mr. Courtney was released in his own custody."

Hanging from the ceiling, a bare forty-Watt bulb lights up my nights. Night comes at six sharp. Every night. Day returns at six sharp. Every morning.

Item:

"Carlton Frott, 32, of Scott's Gully, St. Barnaby, is appearing today in Third Assize Court -- Justice Florian Sturgis presiding -- to plead on a charge of aggravated sexual misconduct during a funeral procession on Swan Lane Monday last. Several outraged female mourners have accused Mr. Frott of seeking sexual gratification by cunningly and persistently rubbing himself against their posteriors. Mr. Frott insists that, overwhelmed with grief, he had merely tried to inch his way closer to the casket to pay his respects to the deceased. The defendant, who later admitted he didn't know the deceased, was once granted a suspended sentence in a similar incident involving church statuary."

The island dozes in mindless serenity, an overgrown chunk of coral sprouting from the scintillating turquoise deep like an oasis in the vastness of the desert.

Today the sea is high, the sky barren. Angry crests collide over cloudy waters. In nature's indulgence you can sense its inventive cruelty.

Old man Godfrey sits on the verandah, shielding his glaucomatous eyes with the back of one hand, scratching Blondie's forever pregnant belly with the other. He is nearly blind but he scans the heavens high above the northwestern horizon, pointing a knotty finger yellowed by nicotine, a toothless, gloating grin upon his face.

"Ah, Flight 902," he chuckles as the jetliner banks leftward on final. Blondie senses elation in Godfrey's strokes. Shooing away her latest litter with a flick of her tail, she rolls on her back and spreads her rear legs farther apart to receive her master's caress.

Godfrey has an interesting occupation. If he smiles it's because every planeload, he reckons, brings a flock of sex-starved white women who pay hard cash for the privilege of being fucked by the uncomplicated youths he has groomed for the occasion, all of them muscular Neanderthals from the highlands who would gladly do it for nothing just to keep score.

Colonel Doulton James, the tall, gaunt, Oxford-bred former chief of Her Majesty's Royal Police, is a steady guest. No one really knows who he does it with -- Godfrey's studs or the prim Québécoises who fly south every year with the geese.

Godfrey rents space from Wingate. They split the profits.

Dolores Wingate leaves her room when the first patrons arrive. She can't bear the moans and the cries of rapture. Walking slowly, feigning sobriety, she sits by the water's edge, alone. The horizon makes no sound at all so she stares at it until she hears nothing but the sea.

High tide. Low tide. Should the ebbing cease, you tell yourself, so will your pulse. Life oozes by. You do not live it; you let it feast on you.

Then there are nights. No, they're not all foretold by fiery sunsets and the smell of nutmeg wafting on the wings of an errant breeze. You soon discover a new kind of blackness, beguiling and ominous where exquisite and chilling dreams compete for a share of your being, nights spent in alternating states of suffocating boredom and unease. Shut your eyes. Hold your breath. Listen to your heartbeat. It often is the only sound you recognize.

Drink yourself silly. Like Brooks. Or fill your lungs with burning ganja, as half the island does when no one looks. Indulge in other pleasures if you can find them, endure them. Lust, like a predator, feeds upon the weak, the lonely, the lost. Deliverance lies ahead, at the far end of a mirror in which you see yourself. No, nights do not beget morning. They're one-way voyages. Everything must end with them when you surrender to your dreams. As you disembark, another flotilla hoists the mainsails, weighs anchor and hazards out of port into Mother Sea's embrace.

Reena. You can't see her in the dark but the black satin form writhing in your arms substantiates her existence. She is real, like the night that engulfs her. Clouds disperse, letting moonlight in through the open shutters. Her eyes shimmer like speckled diamonds but she winces and her ivory smile turns to grimace. It's hard to tell if it's pleasure or pain.

She swears it's okay through the eighth month, and you know she's lying, but you push harder, seeking to go in deeper yet, plowing her life-bearing young body, overlooking the gamy odors, thinking of someone else until the images fade away one by one as you feel yourself coming.

"... I say, that's nothing, nothing at all. Why, on the savanna -- yes I spent a fortnight in Basutoland last fall. Oh, I know they don't call it that anymore, but who can keep track? So many new nations, you know. Every jungle outpost wants its own pennant. Every reformed cannibal yearns for an ambassadorship to the United Nations. As I was saying -- now, was it Basutoland? Yes. Dreadful climate, you know. Why, I found a tarantula snuggling in a bag of bonbons I'd carelessly neglected to secure. Big as my palm, I say, frightfully handsome creature, what...?"

Gwen Peckham cups her hands and wiggles her fingers, spider-like, at Helmut Brunner who nods mechanically and keeps eating. Brunner does not partake of food. He attacks it as if it were still endowed with life.

"... Heavens to Horatio Hornblower, in Tashkent one summer night -- or was it in -- oh, never mind. Anyway, I was stalked by a vampire bat who took peculiar interest in my chignon. Luckily, I wasn't wearing it at the time. You know, bats are so very fond of hair, what?"

Brooks gags as he belches and yawns simultaneously.

Was it Reena? I'm not sure. Maybe it was Rose or Regina or Rebecca or Ruth. It's hard to remember all the monikers they assume. Pick her up at the House of Limbo where young girls give themselves for a meal, a hot shower, a clean bed and the short-lived illusion that love can somehow be kindled by raw, savage sex. Show her a good time. Treat her with kindness. You'll find the experience ennobling. Kindness has a way of humanizing exploitation. No need to pay for your pleasure. Buy her some groceries instead. Hers is a risky occupation and there are at least five other mouths to feed back at the shack on Briton Hill. The one-room hovel is filled with precious dreams, I know, but they will never get past the single window that overlooks the sea where dreams are born.

In these parts a window is like a movie screen on which are projected snippets of immovable, remote reality.

Then morning returns and the sun blazes through dawn's chill dampness. The sea is at your feet and hummingbirds drink from the passionflowers. A new day rises. Think of Tantalus and bite into life as if it were Eden's last fruit.

Pot-bellied, hook-nosed and bronze-skinned like his cousin Rajiv from Poona, Ephraim Wingate, *né* Gupta, gets high on premium gin. His British upbringing demands it. When he's had one too many and he's in the mood to talk, you can forget his cantankerous side. Every man has deep within him a trace of innocence and Wingate's surfaces when he imbibes, a pastime that begins before noon in the shade of his beloved fig tree and continues late into the night until someone carries him to bed.

His stories are laced with bittersweet remembrances of a squandered youth, hurricanes and U-boat sightings off North Point, of volcanic eruptions and moonlit picnics by the reef at low tide, in the nude. You embark with him on the decks of rum-runners and shrimp boats, and sail with their loathsome crews and the hideous harlots they bring on board. He revels in the memory of countless trysts with women of opulent proportions for whom he donned grotesque rubber dildos, many of which are still on display in the bar next to the Queen's official portrait.

In her room since dusk, Dolores Wingate, who has heard it all, drowns her shame in a fifth of Bourbon and sings herself softly to sleep.

On this ocarina-shaped little coral speck, rumors spread like the clap. The official press remains crassly unconcerned and only the outlawed but widely circulated Onyx dares tell it like it is. I write for it under a pseudonym.

The whites, few as they are, perambulate toward extinction. Outnumbered, cut off from the rest of society, they live on windswept knolls overlooking the sea, well above the rickety tar-roofed cottages that hug the dusty road below, and they peer at the blue expanse longingly as if the Union Jack still plied the deep. An hour before dusk, they gather on their terraces and sip tea with lime. Lime is a very sour fruit, even in paradise.

Item:

"New Zealand film producer and world-famed magician Don Drew is stranded on Stonewall, poorer by ten thousand dollars, or so he claims.

"Drew landed here on April 9 from Bigoudi, via Puerto-Diablo where he changed planes and where he asserts he was prevented from retrieving a briefcase containing ten thousand dollars which he 'inadvertently' left on board the aircraft.

"Drew said that airlines are liable for up to five hundred dollars for passengers' losses. He demanded that he be immediately compensated pending restitution of the remainder of the missing cash.

"Flat broke, Drew has contacted the local Muskrat Lodge and was promptly offered temporary shelter by one of its members. Drew has since been summoned to appear at the Immigration Office, a request he called 'tantamount to bullying.'

"Inspector Lionel Hendricks confirmed summoning Drew but insists that it is routine to conduct random checks on foreigners entering Stonewall."

Item:

"'In coming to the aid of film producer and magician Don Drew, the Benevolent Order of Muskrats acted promptly to help a brother in distress,' Hugh Hale, a Muskrat spokesman said yesterday. Noting that the Muskrats do not normally offer charity to their members, Mr. Hale said that when asked, Drew was unable to produce 'any evidence of membership, past or present in a Muskrat lodge, anywhere in the world. Nor could he recite the Muskrat Obligation or display the Muskrat secret grip and sign of distress.'

"Mr. Hale went on to say that 'the person described in the Solicitor as a famous magician told a rather extraordinary tale to several of our members, most of whom found it hard to comprehend let alone believe that a grownup carrying a briefcase filled with money could leave it behind -- except if it hadn't existed in the first place.'

"'Our incredulity deepened,' Mr. Hale went on, 'when we learned that Mr. Drew had no credentials or any proof of his alleged renown. The rope trick and disappearing coin act he performed failed to convince us of his prowess as a magician, though they did provide some measure of comic relief. Nevertheless, the Muskrats, imbued with compassion, acted promptly and extended the hospitality of food and shelter to a perfect stranger.'"

Clyde Ng (pronounced *ng'*) was born in Guyana which, for all its shortcomings, must seem like dream heaven compared to the nauseating walled city of Kowloon where his grandparents came from. Ng owns and runs the only Chinese eatery on Stonewall. His cuisine is as Chinese as Great Neck is unpretentious, which is just as well because his clientele is strictly local, and so are the cooks. Forget Pell Street. Forget Grant Avenue.

Ng is tolerable in the dark or when he doesn't burp, pick his teeth or yawn. Bedecked in rippling layers of solid gold around his neck and wrists, he rarely has anything interesting to say -- a blessing in his case, considering that all his teeth are capped with gold, too.

His wife Kina, a pleasantly plump Orinoco bush Indian who went to mission school, says even less. She paints her nails, brushes her long black tresses with slow, languid strokes and plays dominoes.

The Ng visit regularly. Just to kill time. I sleep with Kina when Clyde is out of town. Everybody sleeps with Kina when Clyde is out of town.

The Zanzi Bar. You can smell the sweat and the beer and the urine long before you reach the top of the stairs. Dimly lit, it's Mobile and Mombasa, Yalta and Yokohama, Rotterdam and Rangoon, Gdansk and Guayaquil all rolled into one stinking pit of depravity.

In one corner, a group of beefy, pink-faced Swedish sailors lean against the counter in drunken stupor, waiting their turn to dance or get laid, their eyes screwed on the apish rear-ends that rock and roll by the juke box.

Dance is the most erotic form of self-expression and eroticism is infectious, so every now and then couples leave the dance floor and retire to a windowless alcove behind the unisex lavatory and down onto filthy mattresses where the owner's dogs sleep at closing time. The music doesn't always drown out the grunts and the ululations.

Amid the graffiti, a limerick sums up the truism of the century. Penned in a tight, disciplined script, it cautions against an especially tenacious breed of body lice, the kind that is "a pain in the groin to get rid of." It is signed by one Jonathan Morris-Moore.

Mr. Morris-Moore has obviously never been to Khartoum.

Item:

"Immigration officials breathed easier yesterday with the expulsion of Don Drew, a citizen of New Zealand caught in a number of squabbles for nearly a month.

"Drew, a self-styled film producer/magician, gave the media and the authorities a hard-luck story involving the loss of a briefcase containing ten thousand dollars on a flight from Bigoudi to Puerto-Diablo.

"When authorities summoned Drew for what they said was a routine consultation, he refused, claiming he was being 'hounded.' Meanwhile, the TeleCom Office has called in their attorney to deal with staff grievances alleging that Drew had verbally abused several operators while attempting to place collect calls to New York, Auckland, Zagreb and Casablanca, with parties at the other end refusing to accept the charges.

"A formal complaint was subsequently delivered at the south coast bed-and-breakfast where Drew was staying. When asked to vacate the premises, Drew made obscene gestures, threw an overflowing chamber pot at immigration agents and barricaded himself in his room.

"Police were called to remove the locks from the doors. Drew grudgingly paid his bill in a dozen different currencies and agreed to leave.

"The episode ended Monday when, under heavy escort and the watchful eye of armed soldiers, Drew boarded a flight to Amsterdam via Paramaribo.

"The Muskrats, whose aid Drew had sought, have since issued a statement in which Drew is described as a 'cheap crook and a swindler.'"

The ruby sun is sinking. Try not to blink. The fabled "green flash" is as elusive as a fading dream. Should you glimpse the fleeting burst of emerald iridescence, make your wish before night drapes the island in sweet fragrant darkness. If you miss it, come back same time tomorrow and try again. Sometimes, the only remedy against boredom is ritual.

Item:

"Mr. Louis Musgrove, 75, of Split Rock, St. Patrick, received a ten-year jail sentence for sodomizing a goat during recess in full view of the pupils at Bishop Johnson Anglican School for Girls.

"Defending Mr. Musgrove, court-appointed counsel, Sir Oswald Bloomquist entered a plea of not guilty by reason of insanity, asserting that his client had quickly been overcome with deep feelings of contrition and was about to slit the goat's throat and donate the carcass to the school's kitchen when he was apprehended by the school custodian, Mr. Nestor Ogilvie of Felarnum Heights, St. Cecilia.

"Sir Oswald pleaded for clemency, arguing in favor of his client's spontaneous -- 'if somewhat misguided' -- good intentions.

"A last-minute motion to remand Mr. Musgrove to Queen Victoria Asylum was denied. In handing down his verdict, Justice Swathmore Hornblythe, Q.C., expressed his personal sense of relief and noted with magisterial panache that, owing the defendant's age and the length of his sentence, the island's goat population could now resume without fear the existence to which it is destined -- 'goat water stew....'"

When you smell formic acid in the air -- you will one night soon -- turn off the lights everywhere. Flying ants are descending on the island and light attracts them.

Congregating on the ceiling in dense, frenzied clusters, they shed their wings and fall to the ground. They will never fly again. Most will be gone by morning. Shake your clothes and shoes before you put them on. Their mandibles are unforgiving and the irritation lasts for days.

It seems that one of old man Godfrey's boys, after defiling the rest of her anatomy, has conquered the heart of one Marie-Thérèse Lapine, of Chicoutimi, and the two are getting "married" at The Bearded Fig Tree

Rounding up guests and "witnesses" for the impromptu ceremony is a cinch. Godfrey sends his scouts to the beaches, the rum shops, the guest houses and the wharf. The dragnet yields a dozen volunteers who will do or submit to anything with ravenous abandon.

Unkindly regarded by nature, Mademoiselle Lapine is one step beyond homeliness, which accounts for the unprecedented extra ten dollars Godfrey had to offer the young stallion for sticking with it a bit longer.

Poorer but outfitted with a man for one short, irreversible dream, Mademoiselle Lapine will awaken alone in a day or two. She will come to her senses, conclude that you can't put a price tag on a dream, and fly back home for another fifty weeks at the typing pool and Sunday confessions until the itch returns, insistent and unmanageable.

Wingate, a licensed notary public, performs the sham ritual. Then everyone joins in. After a while, it's hard to tell who's doing what to whom.

Dolores Wingate is away at her sister's. Business has been brisk at The Bearded Fig Tree. She will not drink this time. She cries a lot when she is sober.

You won't warm up to Bates right away but don't prejudge him. His story speaks volumes about the frailty of dreams. Accused of treason by Ennis Garrison -- "Uncle" to his adoring fans -- the very man he helped hoist to power, Bates was awakened shortly before dawn, forcibly removed from his bed and escorted to the first plane out of Deception where he lived. He landed in Stonewall with the clothes on his back, leaving behind a villa nestling atop a sandy cove and a sloop that often took him for a day or two of seclusion to the outer rims of Deception's coral archipelago.

Bates now earns his keep doing chores for Wingate. His former station in life has earned him the privilege of eating with the rest of us.

Pushing fifty, Andrew Barrington Bates was born in Sri Lanka -- Ceylon at the time -- of British parents who left mother England, "the better to serve her" and as far away as possible from the grayness of her skies and the tedium of her middle class. He was nineteen when he first went to Manchester to study architecture on a stipend extracted from the Home Office by his father in return for some unspecified favor.

Shortly after his twenty-fourth birthday, Bates married the daughter of a Liverpool barrister. Eleven years and three children later, he walked out on his wife and fell for a ballet dancer who sucked his savings dry, did a *jeté* and split. Tired of the drizzle, yearning for some curry in his veins, Bates accepted a civil service posting on Deception and promptly married the first pretty mulatto he'd laid eyes on, Marcia, the maid who came with the house.

For his part, Ennis Garrison quit school early. He earned money fetching tennis balls for his colonial masters and keeping his cute little black ass clean for Major Fitzhugh down at regimental headquarters.

Marcia produced two boys, both the spitting image of their natural father, and a daughter, somewhat darker than anticipated. Bates knew his Cromwell but eugenics escaped him. He later learned that Garrison, the handsome agitator who shocked the ruling party into surrender, had regularly fucked Marcia and lavished her with assorted gifts for her munificence.

Marcia held the door wide open when Garrison's goons, the feared Weasels, yanked her husband out of bed and threw him on the first plane out of Deception.

They called her Daphne. Brooding all day, she draped the sky with a thick overcast that kept rolling in from the east in menacing formations. The wind rose by mid-afternoon, sending shivers through the palm fronds. Squalls lifted beach sand, sending it crashing against the stone parapet with relentless wrath. Thunder rumbled in the distance in muted tones and lightning clawed at the sky, spattering a black, embattled horizon with a brief milky radiance. By sundown, seized with convulsions, the sky turned colors, churning angry clouds that alternately collided and parted to reveal gashes of starlit blue.

Daphne slammed into us a little after midnight at high tide. The assault was merciless. She ripped into the shore, uprooting trees, pulverizing dikes and sea walls. The verandah collapsed. The tin roof was upended. Half the beach caved in and a thick, bubbling sandy bog invaded The Bearded Fig Tree's lower quarters.

Blondie was found floating in the dry well near the tool shed. Brooks was decapitated when a sheet of corrugated roofing tore off the bar and flew into him. Crabs were feasting inside him when we unearthed his headless body in the morning.

Heeding the radio station's advisories, Wingate, old man Godfrey and Gwen Peckham had fled inland to Campbell's Summit. Protected by high, barren ridges, their refuge sustained little damage. Bates, young Brunner and I stayed behind, drawn perhaps by the spectacle of Daphne's magnificent fury. Dolores rode the storm at her sister's cottage on Graham's Landing.

My friend, Max Pontifex, who had not visited for days, later told me he'd taken refuge not on high ground, as disaster preparedness wardens had instructed, but in the flimsy hunters' blind he'd erected in the mangrove and where he often spent the night.

"If I must die, let the sea be my grave," Max had proclaimed with his usual swagger.

Brook's death went largely unnoticed. What with the repairs and the mess to clean up, no one paid much attention when his remains were carted away to a potter's field where unclaimed bodies are interred. That's what his folks in East Hampton had wanted.

Back from her sister's, Dolores immediately drowned the news of Brook's death in a quart of whiskey that took her system three days to distill. She didn't shed a tear. It was her way of celebrating the deliverance of a kindred spirit.

"I adore exotic cuisine. My favorite is God's tongue, or Qx, as the Wanambudu call it. Imagine a large pink slug adorned with markings that resemble a pair of human eyes, each set in a red triangle. How very Masonic.... What? Yes, actually, Qx has a crunchy sort of gumminess to it. Think of caramelized anchovy and headcheese; or pigs' knuckles in aspic. You must try it sometime. I'm also quite fond of rattlesnake. Had some in a Yuma cantina one blistering afternoon. Siberian yak, you say? Why, of course. I was dining with General Fyodor Gregoritchnikov when I first sampled it. Did I ever tell you about dear old Fyodor? No? Ah, what a charmer. Such a good listener. So attentive. He never interrupted me, though he did fall asleep once or twice, the dear fellow. But you know, generals are such busy men. I'll never forget the day we first met in Saint-Tropez. We were both so very young. He was a mere lieutenant then. I was vacationing with Aunt Trudy, may she rest in peace. Yes, well, Fyodor gave me a yak hair comforter when we parted. Must have come from the beast we had just dined on, ho ho ho, what? I'm still mad about it after all these years. I take it to Minneapolis every spring. It keeps me warm. Would you believe I once had to wear my mink coat, gloves and a scarf in Minneapolis in mid-June? Dreadfully cold it was, you know. It seems Minneapolis never escaped the Ice Age. I remember cutting my visit short and booking a flight to St. Kitts that very same afternoon. My friend Gladys -- the one from Minneapolis -- was mortified, poor woman. She even called the weather bureau and complained.

"Have you ever been to Patagonia? No? Rotten climate, I say. Not unlike Newfoundland. Reminds me of the Orkneys, you know. Well, it'll soon be time to move on. Helga is expecting me in Hamburg next week. We're flying to Mogador for a fortnight. The desert air will do us good. Hamburg is so damp, *nicht war?*"

Helmut Brunner, who has just finished scraping a soup bone clean, marrow and all, with his bare teeth, is about to answer but Gwendolyn Peckham has no patience for trivia so she goes on to recount that fateful day in the Congo when a Pygmy mistook her plumed pith helmet for a bird of paradise and shot poisoned arrows at her through the brush.

Item:

"Prime Minister Ennis Garrison has flatly denied rumors that Deception has become 'the epicenter of regional espionage activity' in recent months.

"In a similar communiqué, opposition leader, Foreign Minister Lewis Sandiford Malta, labeled allegations of irregularities by members of his cabinet as 'ludicrous and demented,' and warned that 'rumor-mongers and slanderers' would be unmasked and prosecuted."

Trebor Wirst, editor and publisher of the Solicitor, is a man of refinement and wit. His logic and insights slash through bombast and oratory, and his arguments seldom leave any wiggle room.

Every once in a while, when his hormones act up, when his negritude resurfaces and peels away the gilt of a Cambridge education, Wirst can be expected to deliver one of his legendary broadsides. There are a hundred counterpoints, a thousand repartees, but you find none that appeases your conscience. So you listen politely until he calms down. It's the least you can do for a useful if moody colleague.

"Come now, you can't expect us to survive on raw sugar, nutmeg and saffron, rum and molasses and a rare goodwill visit by the Queen Mum, can you? Sure, we control fifty-one percent of the bauxite mining rights. So what? We have one of the highest density populations on earth. Our trade deficit triples every nine months and the Commonwealth, which had steadfastly shouldered our debt, is itself nearly bankrupt.

"The Regional Common Market? What a farce! We still can't agree on a permanent capital -- though there are more contenders than crabs up a whore's ass. All this makes for lofty parliamentary debate back at Whitehall but nothing ever gets done. Taking sides doesn't help. Yes, we could live by another set of dreams for a while but the granaries would still be half-empty and the police would step up their gruesome witch-hunts.

"So, we invite the world. And every time a plane touches down at Waring Field, with every cruise ship full of chic bleached blondes and white-shod tycoons climbing down the gangplank, we put on our affable, soft-spoken, smiling native faces. Exoticism has a way of camouflaging poverty and political sleaze. So they come back. Then they send their friends and relatives. Word gets around and they all return. Their parenthetical sojourn in 'paradise' guarantees us a permanent listing in the travel guides. It helps us keep our flag unfurled.

"We just can't do without these hordes of part-time interlopers. Our very dreams belong to them. If this goes on, we may never learn what it is we *can* do without them. We shall forever live in fear that someday, someone else will decide to rearrange our reality. It won't be what we had in mind, what we'd hoped for. The weak and the insolvent must make do with a less obliging reality than most, isn't that right?"

Cop out. Breaking out of bondage is the work of heroes. Freedom is expensive; some forms of servitude last forever. The shackles that once bound wrists and ankles can ensnare souls. Weigh the alternatives. Don't procrastinate. It may be time to turn off the lights when you finally make up your mind. You might not be sleepy yet but who are you to argue with the final curfew?

Low tide. Sharma's nubile body glistens through the water. Her cinder-hued skin feels like wet porcelain and her buttocks, firm and spirited, rest against your thighs as her legs encircle your waist. Hardened by lust, her purple nipples press against your chest.

You take her that way, far from shore, your feet firmly anchored in the soft silt-like sand lining the shallow lagoon.

Facing the sea, feeling her warmth through your veins, you look past her searching eyes until the last wave of pleasure tells you it's time to thank Sharma and head back to shore.

Max Pontifex was a master of the epigram, of the off-the-cuff one-liner. He kept large land crabs in a cistern in the lush orchard behind his house on Rock Hall Terrace. He used them for bait and fed them scraps of fish he'd caught earlier in the day.

"It gives the crabs a chance to get even -- in advance," Max had remarked without a trace of sarcasm.

Reliving Stonewall, even in my dreams, forces me to exhume Max, my old friend, my alter ego, the man whose deceptive serenity and lack of pretense I envied above all virtues from the moment our lives intersected and merged.

Max was unkempt and eccentric and anarchic and petulant, but he never came empty-handed. There were always blushing mangoes, tangy tamarinds and other very special treats in his knapsack: turtle soup, fried conch in ginger and saffron, broiled plover breasts stuffed with avocado, to name a few of the delicacies he lavished on me.

But let me tell you about Max.

I'd been fishing that morning, or trying to. Waist-high in water, I'd landed no more than seaweed. Then came Max, wading toward shore, an old rowboat in tow. A straw hat, grimy and frayed, obscured his face, save for the leathered, jutting cheekbones and large, sad eyes, blue like tempered steel. Fixed somewhere on the open sea, they gleamed like the eyes of a man possessed or racked with fever. I will never forget those eyes, the crooked teeth, the untrimmed beard, the scars that tilled his face, the strong, gnarled, skillful hands, the jutting blue veins that tunneled under his sun-bleached pink Scottish skin.

The rowboat brimmed with fish and I suddenly felt like a schmuck with my expensive fiberglass rod and reel and the piece of salami dangling from the hook.

"Some catch," I ventured. "How far out do you go?"

"Not far. Up yonder."

"Up *yonder*?" I would soon master the subtleties of linguistic ambiguity. "Up yonder," like "over dee hill," "up dee road" and "round dee bend," are not precise indicators of distance. Perhaps where time is as elastic as it is on Stonewall, near and far have no real meaning. When I later lived in Central America, I would learn to cope with yet another oddity: the absence of street names or numbers. A common address, I recall, went something like this: Two hundred [meters] south, fifty [meters] east of Lupe's shop. Turn right at the yellow house with the black Chihuahua, then left at José's gas station. That's assuming you knew how to get to Lupe's shop.

"Yes, by the reef." Max pointed to a darker patch of sea three hundred feet from shore.

"What do you use?"

Max held up a battered plastic Clorox bottle and a coil of 20-pound test line.

"What about bait?"

Max pointed to a large tin. "Sea cat" [octopus in our parlance] "and chum." Max removed the lid from a pail in which simmered a rotting bouillabaisse of squashed squid, crushed crab and other putrefying morsels of aquatic life.

"Can I join you sometime? I'll gladly pay you for your

trouble."

Max studied me for a moment, took a deep puff from his cigarette, snorted and spat in the water.

"Tell you what. Meet me by Hartley's tomorrow at five. We'll...."

"Five... uh... in the morning?"

Max's eyes narrowed. A hint of sarcasm animated a tentative smile.

"Is that a problem?"

"No, no, no," I muttered. Five is fine."

"Another thing. Keep your money. Just share your catch." Max eyed my state-of-the-art rod and reel and grinned. "That's if you catch anything." He then turned solemn. "You gotta swear you can swim, man, and won't puke in my boat or I'll toss you overboard like bilge water."

I swore and we were friends, and we left with the morning tide and the catch was abundant. I gave Max my meager take.

"Sorry, I don't eat fish."

Max scowled. He said that killing an animal and not eating it is a senseless pastime. He may have been unkempt and eccentric but he related to animals. He was less tolerant of men. It was difficult not to like him.

Max understood animals: they reminded him of his untamed self. He'd adopted nine dogs and seven cats, all strays. He bred tropical fish and exotic birds, and played mother to a capuchin monkey and a pair of surly macaws that would have gladly scratched each other's eyes out had Max not taken the precaution to house them in separate cages. He also tended to a herd of giant tortoises, a brood of somnolent iguanas and a mongoose that would eventually claim a chunk of his left pinkie.

His favorite creatures, I would soon realize, were the land crabs. Earth-gray, some nearly a foot wide, their claws are bigger than a man's hand and they can crush a toe or snap a finger clean off the joint as if it were a twig. Crabs have one thing in common. They're antisocial and territorial. Every so often, when they feel the urge, they seek out an adversary and fight to the finish. There is rarely a victor in such contests, only lifeless shards of carapace and severed, quivering limbs. Max said that man is descended from crabs; or sharks. He wasn't sure. Max was not always in a generous mood.

Item:

"A Librana Airways plane exploded off Bathsheba's jagged coast shortly after takeoff from Waring Field. All 73 passengers and crew are presumed to have perished. The Coast Guard has dispatched a cutter and divers are now scouring the crash site.

"Several area residents said they were awakened by a loud conflagration at about four in the morning. Mr. Ambrose Fletcher, keeper of the North Point lighthouse, reported seeing flaming debris hurtling toward the sea from an altitude of about one thousand feet.

"An investigation is now underway. No official statement will be issued until fragments from the ill-fated aircraft are recovered. The four-engine DC-8 jetliner had been refueled and was reportedly en route to Santiago when it burst in midair.

"Airport officials here say refueling took place uneventfully under the supervision of two Librana Airways ground personnel. The rest of the crew did not deplane during the hour-long stopover."

Item.

"Downed in a fiery explosion yesterday, Librana Airways Flight 455 was sabotaged. So allege investigators who, sifting through the wreckage, found traces of Semptex and remnants of a timing device taped to a shard of tubing identified as the main fuel line.

"Seventy-three mangled bodies have been recovered, all burned beyond recognition."

Item.

"Investigators now report that the doomed Librana Airways DC-8 aircraft that exploded and crashed off the Bathsheba coast had failed to file a flight plan and was operating under night visual flight rules before it landed in Stonewall.

"It was further revealed that the control tower at Waring Field had not picked up the inbound plane until it entered Stonewall's airspace, well below the pattern, and requested landing instructions.

"Authorities believe the plane had been skimming the ocean surface for a distance of about a hundred nautical miles to the southwest to avoid radar detection.

"The motive for this stratagem has not been elucidated."

Item:

"Deception Prime Minister Ennis Garrison has reported sighting a 'covey' of flying saucers hovering over the ministerial mansion and has instructed his ambassador at the United World League to request an emergency meeting of the Security Conclave.

"Taking note of P. M. Garrison's plea, United World League Secretary General Olatunji Illabobo conveyed his sympathy and assured Deception's head of state that the matter would be addressed when the world body reconvenes after summer recess.

"An independent dispatch filed by our special correspondent on Deception confirms large formations of migratory birds vectored on a southerly course and transiting for a brief rest on the island's coastal marshlands."

The moon is high. You can hear the snarls and the whimpers, the wails and the howls as a pack of feral dogs saunter out of the shadows to copulate on the open road.

Sometimes there aren't enough bitches to go around so the males lose patience and mount each other. So much for the fiction that homosexuality is the sole province of humans.

Move toward them. Vulnerable, galvanized by fear, roused by lust, they freeze and stare, baring angry fangs. Clap your hands once or twice. They disperse and night swallows them.

Find me. Look for the sign, beyond the breadfruit and the almond trees. You're not here to dream but you must find a way.

Fear is such an ugly emotion.

Item:

"Two men, one from Broome Hill, St. Peter, and the other from Irish Gulley, St. Ann, were jailed at the Fortress Prison. Each drew a 90-day sentence.

"Marshall Winston, 27, a car washer, and Olivier Smythe, 24, unemployed, appeared on separate charges. Winston pleaded guilty to using indecent language, resisting arrest and assaulting a police officer. He was separately charged with loitering. Smythe was charged with masturbating on Palmetto Lane and urging a group of visiting Southern Baptist church members to take his picture.

"Both cases were prosecuted by Sgt. Bingham Leonard in District A Criminal Court before Magistrate Coleman Grant.

"In the same court, murder suspect Gloria Prince, of Licorish Village, St. Andrew, made a second appearance. She is accused of murdering her common-law husband, Victor Milling last April. Ms. Prince alleges that Milling fathered five of her seven children but refused to contribute to their support."

Item:

"Former Deception Prime Minister Ennis Garrison, who disappeared under mysterious circumstance two weeks ago after the collapse of his government, is now a guest at an unnamed psychiatric institution in the United States, a reliable source revealed yesterday on condition of anonymity.

"Garrison was thought to have been eliminated when rebels led by Morris Cardinal launched a surprise pre-dawn attack on Deception. The former Deception leader, an incongruous cross between 'Papa Doc' Duvalier and Idi Amin (Dada), is said to be entertaining other inmates with accounts of UFO encounters and excursions in space in the company of winged angels.

"The informant has declined to confirm or deny whether Mr. Garrison had been secreted out of Deception. An independent press contact suggested that 'the likelihood of U.S. involvement cannot be written off.' He cited America's 'historic propensity for giving shelter to political renegades and misfits, war criminals, spies and deposed dictators, or to surgically alter their appearance and arrange for a prosperous and serene retirement in a debtor client-state.'

"The informant further alleged that Garrison is suffering from dementia praecox, possibly the aftermath of an irreversible syphilitic infection of long duration."

So Bates gave Wingate notice. He promised he'd tend to the few remaining chores and thanked him for his hospitality. Wingate toasted the news in his customary fashion that evening and Bates helped him back to his room and tucked him in bed as he'd done so many times before.

On the morning of the fifth, Bates flew to Miami where he'd obtained a professorship in architecture at one of the state's universities. Deception was far behind him. He'd itched for something new. If there's nothing quite as maddening as a persistent itch, nothing gives as much pleasure as a good scratch. Cromwell notwithstanding.

Bates died of a massive heart attack in 1988.

And then, one day, Max, the man I thought I always wanted -- but never had the courage -- to be, Max, with glints of Jesus and Robinson Crusoe flashing from his steely blue eyes, Max, philosopher and fisherman, Max, my good old friend, was dying. I knew the end was near when he saw me off before Christmas, offering me a hollow, almost brittle handshake, his once inexhaustible rucksack now empty, insanity and looming death etched upon his face, disdain and resignation dominating his distant gaze. The transformation had been swift and obvious. He himself had alluded to it from time to time, describing episodes alternating between "awakenings and dizzying descents into dungeons of despair." It was I who had stubbornly dismissed the warning signs, ignored his chivalrous reticence to elaborate, disregarded the hints and the blunt entreaties. I had selfishly reveled in Max's maturing psychosis, pretending that by poking into the dark corners of his mind we would both be headed to some spiritual Promised Land. In reality, I'd carelessly used Max. He'd been a passport to my own self-discovery. He'd made me lust for a power found only in the dreams of children and madmen, and I'd overlooked his pain by pretending that we were both at play in some cerebral dimension that only the two of us could access.

I'd imagined that neighbors would find his partially mummified remains amid the carcasses of parrots and dogs and cats and tortoises, rats scurrying across the filthy litter where he lay, their excrement flecking his hair and beard, maggots, intoxicated and trapped, thrashing about in his stench-filled room.

I could have predicted his unseemly end. His once pristine hilltop home was a shambles and the skeletonized remains of the animals he had raised and collected lay pell-mell throughout the house. His eyes had acquired that glossy, pitiable, distant look of madness.

Max had once said, "Death ain't no cure for madness." It had come, as did all his non-sequiturs, from nowhere, unsolicited and out of context as we fished silently for conger at the edge of the reef. "No," he'd added, his eyes fixed on the horizon as sunset's widening crimson stain splashed the sea before us, "sanity begins at the far end of eternal sleep."

I remember asking him to elaborate but he'd shrugged his shoulders, snorted and spat in the water, as if to consecrate the impending capture of a nightmarish creature, fanged jaws snapping idly at the air, slime dripping from its writhing snakelike body.

"Take congers," Max said, laughing nervously. "They have no friends, you know. We're lucky you and I, we have each other," he added, a primeval fear gripping his voice as the machete rose and fell, decapitating the hideous monster of the deep.

I had over-dramatized my friend's demise, but not by much. Max and the woman who'd mothered him since infancy -- he'd called her "Auntie," both made a slow but irrevocable descent into poverty. The woman eventually died. Max survived, malnourished, slovenly. Eccentricities turned to recklessness. He chain-smoked, antagonized his friends, nettled his detractors.

"I'm mad between long intervals of horrible sanity," he'd once blurted out. "I feel no pain when madness crests." His fleeting but intense bouts of lunacy, it was widely believed, were triggered by alcohol, speed and Valium washed down with Coca Cola. His excesses had become part of the gossip of Stonewall.

"This chap is self-destructing."

One day, as he staggered in a delirious state on the streets of the small east coast village where he'd been given refuge, Max passed out and collapsed. Bleeding profusely from a wound to his skull, he was found by a passerby and rushed by ambulance to a local hospital. He died a couple of days later at the age of 62. The autopsy listed lung cancer and bronchogenic carcinoma of the brain as the main causes of death. He was buried a week later in an unmarked grave.

That year, 1998, the Lunar Prospector found evidence of frozen water near the Moon's poles; cosmologists asserted that the universe's rate of expansion is increasing. Osama bin Laden issued a fatwa, declaring *jihad* against Jews and *Crusaders*. Linked to him, a series of explosions at U.S. Embassies in Kenya and Tanzania killed 224 people and injured more than 4,500.

As Max is laid to rest, nineteen European nations sign a treaty banning human cloning. Unfettered reproduction, even if it results in monsters and madmen, is sanctioned by the Church.

A framed picture of Max adorns one of my walls. A straw hat cockily crowns his shoulder-length hair. Slung over his left arm is a backpack filled with goodies, His right hand, held close against his bosom, restrains a fawn and tan spider monkey. Feigning half a smile, Max's blue eyes seem to focus on mine from any angle in the room. When I look at them I see myself. Max may have been unkempt and eccentric but he made dreaming worthwhile.

If Max looms slightly larger-than-life, or mythic in stature, perhaps even more ethereal in his jarring earthiness, it's because he was flesh and blood, not legend. Reassuringly, that did not prevent him from assuming allegorical dimensions after his death. Those who knew him still speak of him, some with guarded awe, others with aversion. Some saw him as a tormented man; others as a half-witted buffoon. Those who only heard of the barefoot motorbike-riding, shotgun-toting hippie who preferred animals to the company of men still refer to him at the Birdman of Graeme Hall.

I'd ridden on the back of Max's motorcycle, napped on the veranda of his pink coral house and marveled at his animal collections. I'd even spent time with him at the swamp. He had a wicked sense of humor, a disdain of ostentation, an utter lack of affectation. He became my alter ego in another time and space. When I last saw him in 1986, I knew that some deep psychosis had taken hold of him. His speech was slurred, his gait uncertain. He looked dazed. His once-immaculate home was in a state of disarray. Attempts to contact him after my return to New York were met with silence.

I would never set foot in Stonewall again.

PART TWO
THE STORY BEHIND THE TALES

One Night in Copán

THE OPPOSITE OF SILENCE

A need to tell and hear stories is essential to the human species....
The opposite of silence leads quickly to narrative, and the sound of
story is the dominant sound of our lives, from the small accounts of
our day's events to the vast incommunicable constructs of
psychopaths.
Reynolds Price (1933-2011)

What most of us can ever hope to know for certain is second-hand knowledge endlessly retold, recast and misread: the idiosyncratic, hand-me-down robotic indoctrinations of our parents; the expedient reinterpretations of history; the often-slanted pedagogy of our teachers; the fanciful credos of religion; the partisan reflections of the press; and the falsehearted proclamations of our elected officials. What was once learned from instinct and direct personal experience has since been prepackaged into a one-size-fits-all view of the world suitably tinted to accommodate individual preconceptions, partialities and traditions -- not to debunk them. The clarity of truth is being mercilessly dimmed by the tendency to regard it as a doubt-free black-or-white affair lacking grays, devoid of ambiguities, even of improbabilities that would stagger the mind if someone took the time to look, to think, to probe, to doubt.

We all need to hear stories. But somehow we're fond only of those that don't dispute our own accounts of reality, that don't threaten our ideological or emotional comfort zones. We've become so anesthetized by sanctioned reality that we overlook the colossal lies that "official" truths conceal. Worse, we don't read between the lines; we refuse to extricate fact from cautionary tale. We allow hints of veracity to color our fantasies, to stimulate our adrenal glands -- we're thrilled by the oblique suggestion of danger, horror or salaciousness so long as these enticements remain abstract, so long as we're surrogates, vicarious onlookers, not partakers. Other people's stories help legitimize our voyeurism. The tales we spin betray our narcissism.

But what is a story? How is it conceived? Is it the product of mental parthenogenesis -- inadvertent, spontaneous reproduction -- like the star-crossed Otto in *Past Imperfect* (or the ill-fated Jesus of Nazareth?), or is it an artifact, the handiwork of converging processes such as ideation, intuition, imagination and revelation? I can only speak for myself. Whatever my stories might say bluntly or convey subliminally, they undergo frequent, sometimes radical permutations, mid-course corrections and unintended reincarnations. Most of them begin as casual brushstrokes on a blank stretch of canvas eager to be filled. They are left to mature on their own as random colors impart life to tentative outlines. A few are premeditated, like a murder or a terrorist attack. Others materialize spontaneously in my dreams or when I put my mind in neutral. All share a common thread: Incongruity, degeneracy and insanity; the insanity of arrogance; the aberration of absurd beliefs; the folly of conformity; the dementia of greed; the paranoia of hatred; the psychosis of racism; the evil of poverty; the obscenity of hunger; the conceit of anthropomorphism; the lunacy of war; the failure (or unwillingness) to concede that incongruity, degeneracy and insanity are at the core of human existence.

Be they tale, improvised reality, social commentary or extended metaphor, stories are like trees. Their roots dig so deep in time and stretch so far into the rich loam of imagination, memory, experience and clairvoyance that their genesis, their *raison d'être*, is not always discernible in the narrative. Likewise, the melancholy fruits their tangled boughs yield often extend beyond the limits of peripheral vision; one simply can't see the forest for the trees.

Should they choose to do so, readers can stop here, retire the book to some dusty shelf, burn it or share it with a friend. Should they prefer to take a closer look at the ideas, musings and nightmares that spawned them, the candid elucidations below might address some of their questions, suspicions or forebodings.

IN DRANOMOS (p. 3).

When I was a young child I remember drawing two strikingly clashing pictures, one of a cold, gloomy, ashen rainy or snowy day, the other of a dazzling summer scene, complete with smiling sun, undulating rays, frolicking birds, all set against a verdant backdrop that included coconut trees and canary-yellow sandy beaches.

In the first picture, as precipitation engulfs the top of the page, the stick figure behind the window is frowning. His arms hang dejectedly by his sides. His narrow crescent moon-shaped head stoops to one side. In the other, the stick boy is smiling. His head is round and beaming. Holding a bouquet of colorful flowers in his hands, his arms reach for the sky. Even his pet stick dog and cat wear an ear-to-ear grin. As I grew up, my drawing skills improved but I never outgrew my aversion to cold and inclement weather. Ironically, I spent most of my adult life in places that have what meteorologists wryly describe as a "continental" climate. While I understood that emotions are not hostage to weather, I often experienced protracted periods of depression during the long, bleak, windy, frigid winters of the northeast where I lived.

That was to change soon after I moved to the desert. At first, the unbroken landscape, the desolation, the immense dome of sky above the pitted greys and mottled browns of distant escarpments, the grotesque Joshua trees, the roving tumbleweeds, the smell of sage, the rolling mirages levitating on the wings of super-heated air, the deafening stillness -- all stirred a sense of awe heightened by the novelty of it all. The newness soon lost its originality, its allure. And the depression returned, this time accompanied every blazing summer by the longing for a passing snow shower, for the perpetual-motion vitality and the glittering lights of the Great White Way, for the fluid choreography of commuters scurrying in Grand Central

Station's main concourse, for the quaint book stores, the museums and the concert halls, for the prospect of intelligent dialogue. The desert is a suffocating, banal, bleak and dreary place that turns men into savages or hermits or lunatics. Its barren soil is fertile ground for the extremist views of xenophobes and racists who believe that the poor are either stupid and unimaginative, or unmotivated and lazy.

TIME FLIES (p. 13).

Immortality (or eternal life) is a concept that being, physically or spiritually, can be extended beyond death for an infinite length of time. Eternal life can also be construed as timeless existence, not known to be achievable according to cutting-edge physics, nor even definable despite millennia of arguments for "endless life" by some religions.

Biochemically, there is no such thing as death, only decay and transition to a different environment, followed by biochemical re-transformation. Fear of death is a built-in and essential part of the survival instinct. The belief in "rebirth" or in successive lives lies in the fear of being "terminated," thereby asserting the continuance of the self as a hedge against non-being. We all seek immortality -- physical, transcendental. We seek refuge in the notion of a self-replenishing future.

Some scientists, futurists and philosophers claim that human physical immortality will be achievable in the latter part of the 21st century. I have my doubts. Biological forms have inherent limitations that medicine and bio-engineering might not overcome. Meanwhile, I support Wittgenstein's interpretation of eternal life: *"If we take eternity to mean not infinite temporal duration but timelessness, then eternal life belongs to those who live in the present."*

DEATH & TRANSFIGURATION (p. 17).

According to the Coalition for the Homeless, the down-and-out population of New York rose to an all-time high in 2011. More than 114,000 people slept in the city's emergency shelters, including 40,000 children. An undetermined number never made it to a shelter or were denied sanctuary for the flimsiest reasons. Thousands of formerly-homeless children and families that had been placed in subsidized housing have since been forced back into homelessness due to state and city budgetary cuts. There are two million homeless children in America. About seven hundred people die every year from exposure to cold in the U.S.

Meanwhile, the rich are getting richer and illegal, immoral and unwinnable wars are still being heavily bankrolled.

PAST IMPERFECT (p. 19).

Astropaleobiology is a new discipline whose primary objective is to find and interpret evidence of former life on other planets and their moons. At some time in the future, astropaleobiology will widen its focus on the origins of life in the Universe. If successful, it could find evidence of intelligent civilizations from the past, perhaps even from billions of years ago. Space exploration will continue to provide science with a means to understand life's origin, evolution and the ultimate fate of the Universe. Sooner or later, it will answer some crucial questions: Are we alone? Is life on, say, Mars, independent of life on Earth? Is life on Earth the result of immutable physical laws and serendipitous biochemical reactions? Or did life travel piggy-back between the planets on errant chunks of rock, ice and streaming clouds of cosmic dust? Answers will eventually include the "when" and "how" of life. What can never be elucidated is "why." Venturing an explanation would take meaninglessness to the heights of absurdity.

IN HIS OWN IMAGE (p. 23).

"I think, therefore I doubt," I'd exclaimed one day as I awoke from a long slumber and shed the last vestiges of forbearance for senseless beliefs. Nine-tenths of my family had perished in Hitler's gas chambers and the "inscrutability" of God's designs, at best an offensive rationale, had since acquired a loathsome aftertaste.

I rejected the notion that man is born sullied by some "primal offense," that pain ennobles the soul and that sentient beings need to be ruled by an arbitrary system of faith-based values and protocols. In religion's imaginary goodness, I discovered not a path to enlightenment but an instrument of deceit and spiritual enslavement. The makeover from compliant fence-straddler to outspoken mutineer was gradual, filled with misgivings. At first, I found religion's mystique inscrutable. I had meandered through its occluded allegories and bizarre canons like an explorer in a strange, uncharted wasteland. I had glimpsed the very faint light that religion claims to shed but found only vast and gloomy shadows. It is in the shadows that my senses, now accustomed to the darkness, caught sight of a glow, a radiant luminosity that rinsed my pupils free of the gritty debris of credulity. I now understood that absurd beliefs (not glaring truths), prejudice and groundless fear (not common sense), threaten humankind and condemn it to eternal bondage.

Like others before me, I had absent-mindedly tolerated sundry propositions and viewpoints along the way, some of which I even peddled, parrot-like, out of stupidity or intellectual sloth. No more.

Who is this "maker" who inflicts (or tolerates) atrocities for the "good that comes from them"? What cunning and irreducible absolute engineers and orchestrates without apparent aim -- or turns a blind eye to -- the paroxysms that convulse his realm? What "intelligent designer" remains stone-silent while the sobs of his creation are never heard? What "ineffable" entity is this, whose ear is inattentive and whose heart is unfaithful to the throngs who grovel at his feet and seek his succor? What cruel despot decrees that his subjects will mutter words not their own, that they will uncritically obey the injunctions of his self-anointed emissaries, tremble at their threats and admonitions, beg and weep and recite guilt-ridden prayers of indebtedness and veneration, all repeated *ad nausea*m, day after day, to a God who never shows his face, never bares his soul, never sheds a tear, never says he's sorry, a God who grants life and, with it, the fear of death?

Eventually, I concluded that "God" is a useless and costly illusion with which I could dispense. And crypto-agnosticism blossomed into overt and liberating atheism.

THE LONGEST NIGHT (p. 27).

Hitler, Stalin, Mao, the Shah of Persia, the ayatollahs of Iran, Saddam Hussein, Muammar Gadhafi, Jim Jones, David Koresh -- all practiced a form of mass hypnosis designed to achieve complementary objectives: unconditional obedience, political or religious chauvinism and hair-trigger reflexes against any real or perceived threat sparked by extraordinary zeal and violence.

People scoff at the notion of mass-hypnosis because most have already been deadened by their parents at home, teachers in school, "spiritual advisers" in houses of worship, by circus-tent Elmer Gantries, by politicians, by glorious slogans and exalted mantras, by national symbols, propaganda, misinformation, disinformation, historical revisionism and outlandish lies.

Subliminal mind control (brainwashing, coercive persua-sion) is also commonly used in marketing. Say it loud enough, often enough, with the solemn conviction that only a shyster can simulate, and you can sell anything from a hare-brained concept to a product that is obsolete the instant it is unveiled. The subconscious power of advertising is such that cleverly scripted commercials can turn a healthy person into a self-diagnosing neurotic suffering from imaginary incontinence, heartburn, flatulence, impotence, psoriasis, bursitis, constipation, depres-sion and dementia. It's all rectal ventriloquism artfully vocalized by corporate swindlers who laugh all the way to the bank.

The vilest use of mass-hypnosis takes place in politics and from the pulpit. Since the dawn of history despots and benevolent rulers alike have recognized that control of their subjects is essential to their governance. Until recently, the capacity to twist and subdue the mind was crude and haphazard. Today, mind manipulation is science fact, not fiction. No longer a rare or arcane form of warfare to be used against the enemy, it has been widespread and practiced openly on hundreds of thousands of people -- men, women, children, minorities, the elderly, prison inmates and mental patients. We're all potential candidates for -- or the slumbering victims of -- some form of brainwashing. When routine indoctrination fails to produce desired results, lobotomy, psycho-surgery, castration, behavior modification, aversion therapy, electro-convulsive shock and direct brain stimulation are at hand.

History and current events demonstrate how the world's major monotheistic religions have attempted to suppress knowledge, science, pleasure, and desire, often condemning nonbelievers to death for defying their canons. Nietzsche prematurely proclaimed the "Death of God." Not only is God still very much alive, but increasingly manipulated by fundamentalists who pose a danger to the human race by demanding faith, belief, obedience and submission, and by promising a non-existent "afterlife" at the expense of the here and now.

THE LONGEST NIGHT is counter-intuitive and deliberately satirical. In the worst of all possible worlds, one in which, say, "Libertarians" are in control, it is not smokers who would suffer persecution but *non*-smokers against whom a perverse reading of the First Amendment would be applied. Because it tolerates the existence and proliferation of undemocratic thought and institutions that promote faith over science, conformism over iconoclasm, conservatism over heterodoxy, traditionalism over progressivism, and religious rigidity over scholarship, "democracy" has a way of creating underdogs: free thinkers, eccentrics, progressives, activists, liberals, the learned, the enlightened.

NEITHER APE NOR ANGEL (p. 31).

In the 1980s, unable to shore up the absurd claims of creation "science" with empirical evidence, anti-Darwinists raring to inject creationism into America's science curriculum devised a new slogan: "Intelligent Design."

At best a pseudo-science, Intelligent Design (ID) is the untested assertion that the universe, the living things that populate it and the ceaseless upheavals they endure are the result of an all-knowing, albeit paranormal, cause or agent, not a freehand process such as natural selection (evolution) or randomness.

Most ID advocates assert that they are searching for evidence of sentient intent in nature without regard to whom or what the designer might be. In private, however, all unambiguously proclaim that the designer is the Christian God. *[Note the accent on Christian. Forget the Yahweh the Jews invented nearly 6,000 years before the Christian era or the Judeo-Christian deity the Muslims adopted and renamed Allah in the 8th century C.E].*

Taken to its incongruous extreme, ID could one day be called on to explain that things fall not because gravity acts upon them, but because a higher intelligence consciously and deliberately pushes them down. Planes crash, they will argue, and buildings collapse and empires rise and fall because these events are preordained by some inscrutable force of "irreducible complexity," with the more vicious among them insisting that these disasters are in fact the consequence of wrathful divine retribution. A large array of phenomena are already similarly attributed to ID -- from wars waged in "God's" name to hunger and loathsome diseases to earthquakes, cyclones and tsunamis -- damned be the laws of science.

Intelligence is variously defined as "mental acuteness," "the skilled use of reason and application of knowledge" and "the ability to think abstractly" (including the capacity to envision the consequences of one's own actions). Thus, ID presupposes two reciprocal attributes: The existence of a gifted (if unknowable) draftsman and an exceptional blueprint from which a useful and efficient prototype can be rendered.

Such inquiry-stifling premise unavoidably raises questions that, so far, ID has been unable to answer:

• What is "intelligent" about a creature that kills for pleasure and breeds itself to extinction? What mental acuteness is displayed by corruptible beings who cling to rival and inflexible doctrines? What common sense is at play among mortals corrupted by greed and addicted to violence? Why are living creatures susceptible to pain? Why are they defenseless against the fury of cataclysms that ID insists are wrought against us "for mysterious reasons" by some capricious supernatural force? What knowledge is skillfully harnessed by entities powerless or brutishly unwilling to learn from their mistakes?

• What measure of intelligence can be ascribed to a "maker" who inflicts or tolerates atrocities for "the good that comes from them"?

• What cunning and irreducible creator orchestrates without apparent aim -- or turns a blind eye to -- the paroxysms that convulse his realm?

• What abstract reasoning inspires a "grand architect" to remain unmoved by sorrow and calamity and the ceaseless suffering of his own blueprint? What justifies such dispassion?

• What Alpha and Omega unleashes scourges that enfeeble, jeopardize and often destroy its own masterwork?

Until irrevocable proof of "Intelligent Design" is put forth (I'm not holding my breath) the concept will more likely be viewed as a clever stratagem cooked up by a new generation of snake-oil marketers who hijack and exploit hopelessly bewildered spirits and subvert them with falsehoods that only blind faith can ever legitimize. ID is not just an alternate theory explaining the advent of "God's" most defective creation. It's a dangerous eccentricity concocted to exact faith by psychological extortion.

When people *need* to believe in something, they cease to think.

As for me, I'm never more certain of my origins than when I look into the soulful eyes of a great ape. I find comfort and a sense of innocence -- long since lost -- in this genesis. It is when I look at myself and examine my fellow Homo sapiens that I worry about the future of the human race. This is one faulty product that can never be recalled.

DREAMFARER (p. 37).

Over the course of the next few decades, NASA plans to send humans back to the Moon, then on to Mars and beyond. In preparation for these perilous, long -- possibly one-way odysseys -- psychologists are exploring the challenges astronauts will face during these demanding missions. Lessons learned from the past, research in extreme environments, including micro-gravity and high radioactivity, training, conditioning, and countermeasures for psychological stress are some of the things the space agency is in the process of addressing.

Longer missions expose astronauts to immense psycholog-ical pressures, depression and interpersonal conflicts as they adjust to being so far away from Earth. Astronauts have been reluctant to admit to mission-related mental or behavioral problems for fear of being grounded. Because behavioral problems can interfere with the success of a mission -- if not doom it -- future astronauts must learn to detect, assess and manage the effects of loneliness, homesickness, claustrophobia and depression. On multi-crew sorties, they must avoid or swiftly resolve interpersonal conflicts. They might die before they ever reach their destination, or perish after they arrive, of exposure, hunger, thirst, boredom, a suffocating longing for Mother Earth and, quite possibly, madness.

THE VAMPIRE STATE (p. 41).

An estimated 100 million children live and often die on city streets around the globe. Victims of dysfunctional families, swept under the rug of political chaos, social turmoil and faltering economies, street kids are the first casualties of a world in disarray. The price they pay for the follies of society is incalculable: hunger, homelessness, harassment, beatings, sexual exploitation, rape, social alienation, arrest without warrant and incarceration without benefit of trial, often in the company of hardened adult felons where the abuse continues. They live in constant fear. Because they often turn to petty crime to survive, use drugs to mitigate the harsh reality of their hostile environment, they are viewed as "vermin." This perception, promoted by the public and exploited by openly belligerent social conservatives, has helped unleash a tide of violence against the world's fastest growing and most vulnerable minority: homeless minors. It is this disquieting and ongoing rush to infanticide, often accommodated by agents of the state and self-appointed enforcers that this dystopia endeavors to expose.

A HARVEST OF SORROWS (p. 45).

Based largely on actual events and personal observations, this story tells about the disenfranchised, the castaways, vagabonds, beggars, drifters, the homeless and the mad, "that passively rotting mass" [Karl Marx] that teems unseen and unheard in the shadows, the shantytowns, the slums that adjoin affluent neighborhoods. As poverty spreads, social scientists are busy splitting hypothetical hair: Is the proliferation of the underclass the result of being poor? Or is being poor the predictable aftermath of a political system that has turned the economy into a "betting parlor," destroyed millions of jobs and devastated household incomes? Although some experts concede that the existence of an underclass is the result of capitalism's exploitative structure, a scheme that values profits over well-being, they seldom address the phenomenon in other than economic terms. Somehow, the obvious -- government ineptitude, greed, corruption, legal loopholes that allow for the greatest concentration of wealth to remain in the hands of a few, indifference, emphasis on the prosperity of private interests at the expense of the many, all the dynamics that ensure the persistent survival and proliferation of the underclass -- elude them.

The wider premise of this story, which is inspired by real events, is that there can be no underclass without privileged elites and that, in a very real sense, ownership is theft. The continued trivializing, harassment and silencing of their poor -- by assassination if necessary -- as is the unwritten strategy of two Central American states where I worked for 12 years, will one day trigger an insurrection. Predictably, unaccustomed to being flouted, engrossed in the preservation of its national interests and prestige, the U.S., the self-appointed "leader of the free world" will swiftly intervene, send in the Marines, restore the plutocrats, rearm the constabularies and double foreign aid, not a cent of which will ever go to restore the dignity and hope of an ever-growing underclass.

THE FOOT FETISH (p. 59).

According to the New Testament *(John 6:53-55)* Jesus is alleged to have proclaimed:

> *"Verily, verily, I say unto you, except ye eat the flesh of the Son of man, and drink his blood, ye have no life in you. Whoso eateth my flesh, and drinketh my blood, has eternal life; and I will raise him up at the last day. For my flesh is meat indeed, and my blood is drink indeed."*

Two thousand years later, the great Mexican muralist, Diego Rivera, declared:

> *"I believe that when man evolves a civilization higher than the mechanized but primitive one he has now, the eating of human flesh will be sanctioned. For then man will have thrown off all of his superstitions and irrational taboos."*

Shades of Soylent Green! Cannibalism, more precisely anthropophagy, is an ancient culinary option that, judging from historical accounts and intermittent news reports, is far from being outmoded. There is compelling evidence that our Neanderthal, Proto-Neolithic and Neolithic forebears indulged in human flesh. Hunger may have driven the first act of cannibalism but, in time, the consumption of human meat, initially an acquired taste, took on socio-cultural dimensions. In addition to providing an extra source of protein, cannibalism -- or the threat of it -- also acted as a deterrent in intertribal conflicts. In some societies, eating one's enemies was supposed to endow the victors with the strength and wisdom of the vanquished.

Contested accusations of ritual cannibalism have been leveled against the 12th century Anasazi culture in the southwest U.S. and the Minoans in Crete. There is anecdotal evidence of cannibalism having been widespread in 16th century Angola, Cameroon and Congo; in Colombia, Mexico, Paraguay and Peru; among the Carib of the Lesser Antilles, as well as in remote areas of the Pacific, including Papua-New Guinea, the

Marquises Islands of Polynesia and New Zealand.

For all its melodramatic character, THE FOOT FETISH was inspired by a real event and taken to its most odious extreme.

Food was scarce during the German occupation of France, which I witnessed, but members of the Resistance and their families seldom wanted. Farmers contributed generously and my father, a physician, received potatoes, leeks, onions, eggs and an occasional wedge of cheese in lieu of honorarium whenever he delivered a baby or tended to sick or wounded comrades. Fresh meat was more difficult to obtain due in part to a shortage of livestock. Hunting was discouraged because shooting guns invariably drew the Germans' attention.

Despite these restrictions, we could count on our weekly allotment: five hundred grams of beef or horsemeat. My mother would remove the meat from the coarse brown paper wrappings, assess freshness by color and smell, and cook it immediately. One day, the deliveryman brought a piece of meat that was unlike any other my mother had ever seen. Pinkish rather than red, the flesh had an unfamiliar consistency and appearance. Worse, it emitted an indescribable pungency and was adorned on one side with a patch of soft, short flaxen hair. Suspicious, my mother asked the man to wait and summoned my father.

"Look at this. What is it?"

My father exploded. It's not *what* but *who*!" He retched. My mother ran out of the house screaming.

The deliveryman turned white and nearly fainted. "What do you mean, *who*," he asked, his eyes big with outrage and disbelief.

"This is part of a human thigh," my father bellowed. "Where did you get it?"

The man mentioned a name.

"Find out where it came from. I demand an answer next

time I see you, you understand? Take this monstrosity with you and bury it."

The facts, as best as I can reconstruct them, are as follows: A poacher had shot and killed a German soldier, cut up usable parts of his body, and distributed them through the underground food network. It is likely that some less enlightened -- or less finicky -- end-users dined on their gruesome ration that week.

As James Carroll writes in Jerusalem, Jerusalem, *"Where accounted for in terms of mimetic rivalry, the law of the jungle, vestigial instincts of the hunt ... or the mere lust for revenge, Homo sapiens, long after living solely by the hunt, found itself still to be at the mercy of the urge to kill."* Perhaps killing is a form of inhibited cannibalism.

Cannibalism is a chilling reminder of our humble and primitive origins in the animal kingdom. To cannibals -- Andrei Chikatilo, Jeffrey Dahmer, Albert Fish and Ed Gein among the most infamous -- human flesh is as appetizing as filet mignon, leg of lamb, shrimp scampi or duck à l'orange. It may be more the result of nurturing, than instinct, that we deem it perfectly normal to kill and eat other animals, while refrain from devouring one-another (except metaphorically, of course, and on the battlefield).

As Richard Routley-Silvan observes in his essay, *In Defense of Cannibalism*, something that is innately repugnant does not make it morally taboo. Moreover, he adds, the fact that we find cannibalism nauseating is probably the outcome of upbringing and habituation rather than an inborn aversion to human flesh.

Bon appétit.

ONE NIGHT IN COPÁN (p. 67).

UFO investigators face daunting challenges. In the absence of "hard data," say, a fragment from a UFO or the remains of a traveler from some distant galaxy, they are left with three choices: stop looking, speculate and infer, or rely solely on eyewitness accounts, which are notoriously unreliable and apt to have been dreamed up by crackpots or fabricated by jokesters with a fondness for mass-induced hysteria.

One of the best known examples of collective panic was the 1938 *"Invasion from Mars"* when Orson Welles' radio broadcast of a science-fiction drama sent thousands of listeners from coast to coast into a state of terror because they believed Martians had landed on Earth and the end of the world was at hand.

In his 1966 analysis of the Welles broadcast, subtitled *A Study in the Psychology of Panic*, social scientist Hadley Cantril suggests that the anxieties of the time, the economic depression and the imminent outbreak of World War II had set the stage for the ensuing public frenzy. He examines the psychological factors that made so many people believe that the events dramatized on the radio were real, whereas others dismissed them as fiction or were astute enough to call the police and newspapers for corroboration. The believers seemed to have a "mindset," a preconceived notion that God was going to end the world and that an invasion was imminent; or they harbored fanciful concepts about the potential of science. When they heard Welles' masterful and chilling adaptation of the *War of the Worlds*, they accepted it as a validation of their own beliefs and mulishly disregarded any evidence that might disprove their apocalyptic fantasies. Others, bereft of standards of critical judgment, showed a dearth of discernment by accepting with quasi-religious fatalism what the broadcast reported as the truth.

Cantril concludes that what these susceptible groups share

are characteristic feelings of personal inadequacy and an inability to rely on their own resources to see them through the darkness of ignorance. They believe their lives and fate *"are very largely dependent on some focus beyond [their] control, or hang on the whim of some supernatural being. All this adds up to an intense feeling of emotional insecurity, one which is likely to be augmented as the situation around them appears more and more threatening. [They] will be highly susceptible to suggestion when they face a situation that taxes their own meager self-reliance, and especially when their emotional security is threatened by official pronouncements such as those coming from a radio station of other public source...."* -- namely a respected Honduran daily newspaper in which the bizarre and utterly fictitious events chronicled in **ONE NIGHT IN COPÁN** were published.

It was a rereading of Cantril's study that inspired the elaborate hoax.

Fellow journalist Pablo Beltrán (not his real name) did conspire to publish the tall story I'd sent him for his amusement. An otherwise serious, melancholy man given to fits of weeping and raging outbursts of anger, Beltrán understood how this would play out among his highly religious, hopelessly superstitious compatriots. In a rare moment of impishness, switching from solemnity to frivolity, he ran two consecutive articles. I did not exaggerate the ruckus and trepidation their publication provoked. A print version of the e-mail correspondence between Beltrán and me, faithfully reproduced in the story, is now under lock and key. Beltrán, who died earlier this year at the age of seventy, took the secret of our devilishly enjoyable prank to the grave.

LET ME TELL YOU ABOUT MAX (p. 79).

This is a story of wanderlust and gloom, self-exile and intrigue, boredom and madness. It is also the story of an improbable, spur-of-the-moment friendship that ended like so many accidental liaisons, the casualty of distance, distraction and death.

Some incidents were dramatized to add epic realism, or compressed to lend them the surreal hue they would eventually acquire on their own. Some names were changed because the characters' real identity was not relevant to the narrative, or because those who spoke off the record needed to remain in the shadows. One notable exception to these necessary evasions is my late friend Max Pontifex.

In my presence and for the ten years or so that we knew each other, Max was kind, generous, easygoing and quite open about the demons that possessed him. But he wasn't evil. I believe that inside the Max who rankled people and abused their patience, lived an anguished adolescent trying to find his place in a world whose conventions he spurned. It is *that* Max to whom I pay tribute. An accurate portrait of the man must necessarily include a depiction of his darker side. It was not my intention to mythologize Max, only to commemorate his brief and tormented existence.

Sorting fact from fancy proved laborious and frustrating. People who could have added crucial details acted with robotic reticence. They hedged, doled out trivial tidbits, gossiped or clammed up. Silence is the simplest form of disinformation. Unlike open scandal, which peaks in an orgy of finger-pointing, then dies, silence leaves a trail of inferences and a scent of putrefaction. Several acquaintances opened up on condition of anonymity. Sometimes the truth can only be bought in exchange for silence. One thing is certain: Few people were as genuinely fond of Max as I was. Some tolerated him -- from a distance. Others feared and loathed him, perhaps because he saw through their pusillanimity, their hypocrisy, their conceit, their bigotry. Others yet, among them close relatives, turned out to have known him only vaguely -- or knew him not at all. For most, Max quickly passed from reality to hyperbole.

Max was born on September 3rd 1939, the son of Keith Overton Pontifex and Doreen Harris, both of Scottish ancestry. There are persistent rumors that Keith and Doreen were not married when Max was born. His blood relatives insist they were but Max told me they were not. For people of their standing on the island, then still a British colony, a child born out of wedlock would have been quite an embarrassment. Doreen was suffering from tuberculosis when she gave birth to Max. Confined to the TB ward of a local hospital, Doreen gave up custody of her son. She died a year later. Max was soon adopted and raised as their own by a prominent and generous family who loved him, pampered him, catered to his whims, indulged his foibles and overlooked his profligacies. Why Max was not reared by members of his own clan is left to conjecture. Their rejection may explain the pent-up antipathy he felt for his blood relatives.

After his wife's death, Keith Sr. remarried and moved to Canada.

Max attended a prestigious school but was soon expelled for sneaking up behind the teacher's desk and releasing a bat under her skirt. Although he was fond of books, he never had much interest in formal studies. During "bird season," he would leave home dressed in his school uniform, head straight to the hunter's blind he'd erected in the swamp -- he'd nicknamed it "Vietnam" -- and where he kept an extra set of clothes. In the evening, after a day of duck hunting and daydreaming in the dense thickets that rose from the tidal shore, he'd put his uniform back on and return home.

Max was in his twenties when he was either coerced or lured to Canada by his father, who promptly put him to work in his gas station. Max, whose way of life did not include anything remotely resembling conventional work, was unhappy pumping gas, washing windshields, changing tires and interacting with people. He did things to annoy his father, who had financed his trip, and whose dubious hospitality he was determined to erode. Once, he pumped gas into the trunk of a car and filled the tank of another with water. Accustomed to walking barefoot since childhood, Max told me how he hated having to wear shoes. He also complained of Canada's bitter winters and stifling, sultry summers. Max missed his island life. He managed to scrape a few dollars for a one-way flight out of Canada. He kissed the ground when he landed back home.

Max's story has an uncanny, fragmented Biblical texture, not unlike the New Testament's clashing renderings of the Jesus of Nazareth mythicized decades apart by biased and unreliable biographers, or the multi-angled perspectives of a crime observed by different eyewitnesses in the Japanese cinematic masterpiece, Rashomon. Somewhere between the lionizing and the demonizing and the blasphemy emerges a portrait of Max everyone seems to recognize.

"I knew Max from my very earliest days. We were neighbors. To call him eccentric is to cheapen the uniqueness of his idiosyncrasies. He was a collector-turned-hoarder. He collected stamps, books, magazines, but his real interest was wild life -- dogs, cats, fish, birds, reptiles. He raised a caiman in his bathtub until it became deformed and grew into a U-shaped monster. His real love was birds; a strange passion for a man who kept wild fowls such as moorhens, budgies, grass finches and parrotlets in captivity when they clearly belonged in the wild. He may have very nearly and singlehandedly driven the island's parrotlet population to extinction. He was a

wildfowler, addicted to the swamp life who exulted during the migratory season when he could shoot various species of North American shore birds headed south for the winter. He was up before dawn in the swamp waiting for the sandpipers to fly in.

"I owe him my life. One day -- I was fourteen -- I joined him at the swamp. As I attempted to cross a stream, I stepped into quicksand. I was making my last gurgling sounds as I sank beneath the mire when Max turned around and pulled me out by my hair. Yet he had a violent temper and once aimed his loaded shotgun at me. I still wonder why he didn't pull the trigger; that had been the intent I'd read in his eyes.

"When Max could no longer fend for himself he was removed from his house and taken to a cottage in the country. What we found in his once-pristine abode was worse than the Augean Stables. Books and magazines were stacked to the ceiling; the stench of rotting food, of decomposing flesh permeated the house with that unmistakable redolence of death.

"His dark side had its own validity. I witnessed his bouts of extreme temper. He was fascinated by living things; he could have been a gifted naturalist. Yet he did perplexing and contradictory things with the animals and birds he kept. The caiman he raised in his bathtub grew so deformed that it had to be euthanized. He was also quite territorial and demonstrated this in ways that are remembered as part of the legend of Max. He captured moorhens in the swamp by stripping naked and wrapping his head in a bundle of weeds and water lilies, and slowly moving on the unsuspecting birds. Once, a group of women from the old white plantocracy were picnicking on a grassy verge in the swamp. Resenting the intrusion, Max resorted to his 'Apocalypse Now' guerrilla tactics. Disguised as a floating aquatic plant, he slid quietly through the water and suddenly emerged, a nude Medusa-like apparition. Startled, the women fled the scene, screaming."

A more laconic portrayal by another acquaintance of his is no less revealing.

"Max suffered from chronic headaches. For twenty years or so he took large doses of Valium. He also abused other drugs, recreationally or to quiet the demons that consumed him. Most people only knew Max the swamp shooter and the animal collector, but not the man. Many held a slanted perspective, more the result of hearsay than direct experience. Others perpetuated the myths that evolved with the passing of time. Yes, he was strange, unconventional and unpredictable. He did a lot of 'shite' and it was easier for people to dismiss him as a madman than as a troubled soul."

A family friend's frosty ruminations -- shared thirteen years after his death but focusing on the last days of his life -- betray a curious lack of empathy:

"Max was a good talker but he was unable or unwilling to do normal things, like shave or get a haircut. He mishandled money. He collected animals but after a while he stopped caring for them. We found dozens of mangy and starving dogs in the yard. The cellars crawled with starving cats and dying birds. The fish tanks, once pristine and thriving with life, reeked with dead fish. The cupboards were bare and what little food we found in the refrigerator had long since rotted away. He was committed to a mental hospital. He was released six months later and he went back to getting high on 'whizz' [amphetamines]. He spent most of his weekly allowance on cigarettes and valium. He gambled the rest away."

Terse and non-committal is this gem from left field offered by a former schoolmate:

"Max liked poetry. His favorite was Alfred Noyes' The Highwayman. He knew it by heart. No wonder. He had to write it five hundred times as punishment in school for some

143

transgression."

Yes, I saw Max's dark side, but I also knew a man who struggled to fit in without having to submit to other people's conformist expectations, to comprehend the world around him by avoiding its most flagrant contradictions. None of us is universally liked. Unconventional ideas and behavior in the very straight-laced "Little England" ambience of "Stonewall" must surely have set tongues wagging, caused friction, pitted fans and detractors.

Asking too many questions on a small island that pulls in its sidewalks at dusk and spends the night gossiping about friend, kin and foe is as foolhardy as it is pointless. Efforts to shed light on the dimmest features of a terrorist incident that would invite international condemnation required that I settle on the fragmentary details I was able to exhume from a mass grave of cover-ups, half-truths, hearsay, gossip and lies.

What I learned has since entered the public domain: On October 6, 1976, eleven minutes after takeoff from Barbados, Jamaica-bound Cubana Flight 455 exploded at 18,000 feet. All 78 people on board were killed in what was then the deadliest terrorist airline attack in the Western hemisphere.

Evidence implicated several CIA-linked anti-Castro Cuban exiles and members of the Venezuelan secret police. Declassified CIA documents indicate that the agency "had concrete advance intelligence ... on plans by Cuban exile terrorist groups to bring down a Cubana airliner."

Four men were arrested and tried in Venezuela: Freddy Lugo and Hernán Ricardo Lozano were sentenced to 20-year prison terms. CIA operative Orlando Bosch was acquitted on technical grounds and pardoned despite objections by President H. W. Bush's own Defense Department which insisted that

Bosch was one of the most deadly terrorists working "within the hemisphere." He died in Florida in April 2011.

Luis Posada Carriles was held for eight years while awaiting final sentence. He managed to escape and entered the U.S., some say, with the help of CIA cronies who bribed Venezuelan authorities. He was held on charges of entering the U.S. illegally and released. Attempts to extradite him were obstructed by then CIA director George H. W. Bush. Posada had a long relationship with the CIA. In 1961 he joined the agency's Brigade 2506 assigned to invade Cuba. He has since been involved in numerous anti-Cuban plots, including the attempted murder of Fidel Castro, the bombing of the British West Indian Airways office in Barbados and the Guyanese Embassy in Trinidad. Posada lives in Miami and is said to receive a $300 monthly "pension" from the CIA, which still considers him of "operational interest." He remains actively involved with right-wing anti-Castro fund-raising groups.

What I could not authenticate was inferred from precedent, circumstantial evidence and the laws of probability. When all else fails, filling in the blanks by reading between the lines is the only way to unearth truths that would otherwise remain entombed.

Last, what LET ME TELL YOU ABOUT MAX attempts to convey is the woeful inaptness of western man to the torpid cadences of life in the tropics, to the provincialism and pettifoggery, the dogmatism and the clannishness, how susceptible he is to the creeping "bestial affliction" of boredom in the very bosom of paradise and why, over time, he cannot seem to surmount it by any act of will. Too much sun makes people horny. It also predisposes them to indolence, apathy and a diminished sense of urgency or commitment. Also, being white in a predominantly black society no longer ruled by its colonial masters must have its downsides, frustrations and fears. Though Max often expressed grave misgivings about the future of "Stonewall," they were mercifully devoid of the veiled but pernicious racism of his fellow whites.

"Stonewall" is a lovely place to visit. I don't see great minds germinating in its lush and colorful setting.

What with its cryptic undertones, allusions and timeline inversions, composing LET ME TELL YOU ABOUT MAX was especially challenging. I am deeply indebted to Peter Reece, Frances Roman and Prof. Karl Watson for their keen sense of recall, their incisive reminiscences and dispassionate elucidations.

POSTSCRIPT

Whoever yearns for freedom, justice, and peace
may rise again and raise his head,
for in Christ liberation is drawing near.
Luke (21:28).

Somehow, that 2,000-year-old pledge turned out to be an empty, cruel ruse. The "Savior" has saved nothing. Convulsing under rising waves of hatred, ignorance, superstition and stupidity, racked by mounting violence, the world still awaits salvation -- from itself. In defiance of halfhearted reprimands by the "First World," racked by poverty, despair, ethnic strife and shifting allegiances, "emergent nations" continue to indulge in genocide. Generation after generation, desperately in need of social justice, economic equilibrium and independence from their puppet-masters, wallowing in apathy and inertia, they teeter on the brink of civil war or have succumbed to it. In other parts of the world people struggle to preserve increasingly shrinking fragments of their ancestral homelands. Climate change puts arctic regions on thin ice, threatens to inundate coastal areas and engulf dozens of islands around the globe, while prairies wither and turn into dustbowls. Embroiled in unwinnable wars, itching for more, the U.S. clings to the two-party-system -- both parties the flip sides of the same tarnished coin, both indistinguishable one from the other except for the partisanships and antipathies they inspire, both tied to corporate wealth, both intent on blocking meaningful reform in the name of Wall Street-dictated crony capitalism, both involved in larceny against the poor.

The gap between the haves and the have not continues to widen. The Catholic Church, the richest empire on earth and the self-anointed moral arbiter to millions, is embroiled in sordid scandals. Living in Babylonian splendor, donning richly festooned vestments, basking in the idolatrous reverence of the flock, the Pope breathes the rarefied air of his own saintly afterlife and sneers at men's earthly needs. Meanwhile, intoxicated by the apocalyptic rants found in Revelation, Evangelical Christians pray for an all-consuming Armageddon.

The crucifixion of Jesus of Nazareth is a fitting metaphor for man's inhumanity. Alas, its commemoration reminds us all that salvation -- like justice, human rights, compassion, ethics and love -- remains a distant vision, not a serious objective.

History is written and retouched by men. One man's truth is another man's propaganda. The allure of history rests not always in the events it chronicles but in the chronicler's subjective interpretations. Without such 'embroidery,' the annals of man would consist of little more than a laconic compendium of facts and dates. Whereas some social scientists tend to interpret history as an evolution from savagery to emotional maturity and intellectual refinement, reality is far less reassuring. In the aggregate, human society seesaws wildly between states of stagnancy, feverish creativity, uneasiness, turmoil and madness. While these oscillations can be blamed on the cretins, killers and kleptocrats we elect (or surrender to), they are hastened, prolonged and fossilized by the appalling lethargy of the populace. As Voltaire wrote, 'history is a lie commonly agreed upon'." Yes, victors write history to justify and exalt conquest, losers to mitigate defeat. Neither side will concede the other's account. The hostility such divergence of opinion invites leads to other assaults, further setbacks.

In a story, as in a revolution, the most difficult part to invent is the end. In addition to bringing their own knowledge of history, story-tellers must own up to it: an ending is not supposed to be a surprise. To envision a plausible finale we must also reflect on the paroxysms of lunacy and violence that now convulse the planet.

THE END STORY

"On that day, dust possesses the earth; on that day,
a blight is on the face of the earth; on that day,
a cloud arises; on that day, things fall to ruin;
on that day, the tender leaf
is destroyed; on that day, the dying eyes are closed...."
The Popol Vuh

Ongoing military conflicts around the world have claimed more than four million lives, civilian and military, in the past 20 years. They continue to result in violent deaths in Afghanistan and Syria, Colombia and Somalia, Mexico and Sudan. Insurgencies and sectarian rivalries in Southeast Asia, Africa and Latin America killed another million people. Five million lives were lost during the Korean War; almost half that many in Vietnam.

One facet of madness is the will to kill for an idea. Technology just makes men more efficient and choleric killers.

The prognosis is poor. Other wars are looming. Some will be too close for comfort. They will be preceded by a salvo of official declarations and counter-statements tailored to help adversaries save face at home while giving the rest of the world the impression that a global conflagration is inevitable unless one side or the other relents.

War is a lucrative pursuit, especially for the war mongers, the bankers and the gun merchants, but they often erupt as a result of baseless fear, miscalculation or overreaction, not conscious design. No one really wants war and no one is quite prepared to wage it, let alone win it. In time, words get sharper, less conciliatory, and weapons, the antithesis of reason, grow deadlier with each sound bite.

A number of wise men whose opinion no one seeks suggest that the capacity to annihilate one another discourages rivals from slugging it out, thus justifying the escalation of that capacity to exponential thresholds. They call it mutually assured destruction; MAD for short. Everyone finds it an amusing little acronym. Few understand the implications.

Other wise men liken hatred to an energy that can't be compressed indefinitely and which must be vented from time to time, thus making a random skirmish, in insurrection, an all-out war, a holocaust a routine if somewhat inelegant necessity, like farting. Subconsciously, humans crave war, the wise men argue. Catharsis or reflex, war helps shake off the unbearable burden of having to fake civility, simulate enlightenment in a world cyclically shamed by ignorance, stupidity, clouded judgment, madness and violence. Wired as he is, the "naked ape" can't forever conceal his homicidal instincts. He needs a user-friendly outlet for his wickedness. Dreaming is not enough.

And so the rhetoric of war escalates in tone and intensity. No one protests very loudly. Not a single voice rises against the demagogues who beat the drums of war. No one dares send to hell the politicians who cheer it on, the economists who justify it, the bankers who finance it, the industries that thrive on it and the generals who prosecute it -- while the rest of us schmucks are forced-marched to the front to die, be maimed or driven crazy in the name of some elusive grand cause. Even the professional dissenters, doctrinaire and often deluded, keep quiet, their intellects anesthetized, their vocal cords deadened by fear or waning conviction. A malignant tedium, a pervasive apathy -- compensated by a lust for blood, anyone's blood -- has replaced common sense.

The late Samuel Huntington was right: When dissimilar ideologies collide or hegemonic interests diverge, pitting cultures against one another, conflicts erupt. The "low-intensity" conflicts that now thunder across the globe confirm the Harvard scholar's thesis. Western (primarily American) imperialistic arrogance, rising Islamic self-identity, overpopulation, spreading poverty and hunger, all have carved an intractable and widening rift between ideological and cultural opposites.

Torn by decades of civil strife, diminishing civil liberties, corruption and dwindling natural resources, some countries will fall first like gangrenous limbs in an orgy of blood-letting that turns the rivers red and meadows into open graves.

Unable to trade with impoverished client states and spurned by their former political partners, some nations crumble under the weight of their own spectacular if short-lived economic gigantism. Self-absorbed, mired in ethnic violence, other nations restart wars they did not have the courage to eschew or end. Isolated and moribund, others yet collapse in a final spasm of paranoia.

In the Middle East, the predictable collapse of a shaky forty-year alliance between two Arab States, a territorially partitioned Palestine and their perennial enemy, Israel, sets the region ablaze. Militarily worn out, economically drained and exasperated by its prevarications and obstructionist policies, the U.S. abandons Israel to its fate. Willful and incorrigible, now armed with nuclear, biological and chemical weapons, Iran stands poised to launch its long-range surface-to-surface missiles.

Dismembered, smoldering and reduced to rubble by religious strife and half a century of U.S. occupation and economic colonialism, Iraq threatens to blow up. A fraudulently elected president had bulldozed America into an undeclared, costly, unpopular, bloody and unwinnable war premised on counterfeit assumptions against an enemy fathered and long coddled by the U.S. Saddam, it will be remembered, had been Uncle Sam's Man in Baghdad until he defied his puppet master's authority. No one in America flinched when this thug massacred thousands of his own people. A dozen warlords, each with an ax to grind, now control small enclaves of half-starving and venal mercenaries, and the debacle lingers on as the U.S. lets itself be dragged into yet another Middle Eastern crusade that dangerously compromises its military capital and lays waste to America's gutted economy.

As the U.S. spreads itself thin in a number of military operations, Russia (which itched to bomb the U.S. in the early stages of the Cold War, and never gave up its desire to do so) seizes the moment and reasserts itself. Russia has nothing to lose should the U.S. eventually "decline and fall" -- on the contrary. Stirred by an ancient longing and mortified that it never recovered from the breakup of its vast empire, Russia now weighs its options and eyes a disintegrating world. The boys in the Kremlin know that Western Europe will blink and do nothing to help the U.S.

Russia also understands that America has lost much of its prestige, preeminence and economic clout; that it is being increasingly isolated as the number and fanaticism of its foes grows with every saber-rattling pronouncement from the White

House. In response to America's anti-ballistic program, Russia rebuilds the most formidable arsenal of nuclear warheads the world has ever seen. North Korea, a sworn enemy of the U.S., produces nuclear weapons and state-of-the-art delivery systems. Much of Western Europe, now weaned from NATO and pursuing its own objectives, turns against the disastrous and unwinnable war in Afghanistan. Islamic nations -- fundamentalist and secular -- turn on the volume in their hatred of the U.S. New terrorist cells are springing around the world as antipathy mounts against globalization and in response to a perception by Muslims (accurate in the narrowest sense) that the U.S. is waging war against Islam.

Africa, still smarting from 500 years of colonization and resentful of America's long-standing indifference toward its unending woes, turns bitterly anti-U.S., anti-western, anti-white. The South African blood bath, long prophesied but never forestalled, even after the abolition of apartheid, erupts like a pustule, inflaming contiguous states and storming through the continent from the Cape of Good Hope to the Mediterranean, from the Indian Ocean to the Atlantic.

Episodic at first, famine spreads like wildfire. Infant mortality skyrockets. There are other casualties. What little food can be scraped to keep the heart pumping proves less than adequate to nourish the brain. Over three billion people suffer irreversible brain damage. Asylums are full. More are desperately needed to contain a swelling tide of insanity but none is being built and the overflow spills into streets, along with the homeless, the sick, the dead and the dying.

After years of uninterrupted fighting, no one knows for sure why wars are being waged. Nor can anyone quite remember why the all-consuming conflicts had erupted in the first place. The belligerence of the warring factions has not abated but the cost of maintaining troops and materiel skyrockets, prompting each side to further slash domestic programs while raising taxes and artificially deepening inflation.

Things aren't much better at home. Men seventeen to fifty-nine are in uniform, training for the front or patrolling the streets. Everyone is armed. In the cities, the haves wrangle with the have not. Looting, assaults and other forms of violence soar during the long hot summer and thousands die at the hands of vigilantes, mercenaries and gangs, all more eager to settle scores than preserve law and order. Justice is blind to injustice. Anti-war activists are on the attack. All they achieve is to foment greater resentment against their cause by flag-waving diehards too old for conscription, a dispensation that always stirs patriotism and raises the decibels of jingoism and sanctimony to ear-blasting levels.

Basic staples -- bread, sugar, eggs -- are in short supply. Meat, when available at black market prices, is rarely fresh. But hunger subverts reason and everyone takes chances. And while hunger and exposure kill the poor, it's often food poisoning that claims those who can still afford to eat.

Not unlike ants, we spend the fall hoarding and digging in deeper. A calamitous winter, at best, lies ahead.

Fusing pseudo-capitalism and Marxist-style collectivism, bloated and prosperous, China smiles like a Cheshire cat and waits.

Find me. I'll be waiting. We'll all be waiting, the dissidents and the insurgents, the heretics, the free thinkers and the idol smashers.

We're all mad; only the very brave or the despairing let go. But we'll keep on feigning sanity. It helps dress up our lives. If acting is the art of pretense, living is the science of deceit. We do a bit of both now and then and sometimes it's hard to tell which is which. As my late friend Max used to say, "We're not God's most perfect creation. In fact, we're quite defective: We keep on multiplying and our offspring come without a warranty."

One Night in Copán

ACKNOWLEDGMENTS

I am indebted to my parents, learned, urbane, fair-minded and liberal, for instilling a love of books and an appreciation for music, art and philosophy, for sparing me the enslavement of religious indoctrination and for enduring, if not always endorsing, my wildest antics. To my mother, a selfless, unassuming woman of great culture and refinement, I owe my fondness for beauty and symmetry. From my father, a loving, iron-willed and incorruptible man who abhorred ostentation and pretense, I learned that self-esteem and a respect for truth offer infinitely greater rewards than a good reputation.

I salute my teachers, those I pleased when I applied myself and those I exasperated when I didn't. Their erudition, pedagogical skills and saintly patience for the lazy, unfocused, mercurial and rebellious student I was helped lay the foundations on which I would erect a lifetime career of endless beginnings.

I can never adequately acknowledge the immense influence a number of prominent writers, poets and philosophers had on the constantly evolving person I would become and, by extension, on the ideas I would champion. Their prose, verses, insights and eye-opening reflections resonate as intensely today as they did in the days of my youth. Most were French: one was denied a Christian funeral for penning vitriolic anti-religious polemics; five were imprisoned, one for denouncing the brutality of colonialism; the other for suggesting that the blind can be taught to read through the sense of touch; the third, the son of a prostitute, for vagabondage, lewd acts and "other offenses against public decency;" the fourth, for stretching the limits of literary freedom in tracts that mixed raw eroticism with civil disobedience. The fifth spoke for the common man and rose with uncommon bravery against government and military corruption.

My other mentors wrote in Arabic, English, Dutch, German, Russian, Sanskrit and Spanish. Three hailed from England; one of them did not survive the spurious puritanism of his Victorian milieu. One died insane -- as do many who seek shelter from the battering storm of reality in the haven of delirium. All were freethinkers, rebels and iconoclasts, now long dead, but whose works and the reformist ideas they impart still inspire new generations of mavericks-in-training.